MISS BRONTË'S DILEMMA

By

Coreen Turner

For

Ursula Wright 1937-2016

Great friend, greatly missed.

CONTENTS

ACKNOWLEDGEMENTS

I have consulted many books, journals, and newspapers while writing this book and would like to acknowledge particularly Margaret Smith: The Letters of Charlotte Brontë; Juliet Barker: The Brontës; Molly Tatchell: Leigh Hunt and his family in Hammersmith; Norman Penty for his genealogical search for the William Smith Williams family, and Leslie Marquand for his study of Lord Byron. In turning these happenings into a novel I have sometimes taken liberties with time and place.

I would also like to thank the following people for advice, encouragement, and sheer hard work: Kevin Bennett, Jean Clymer, Susan Kelly, Jo Leveridge, Annabel Shirt, Chris Walsh and Joan Ward.

ABOUT THE AUTHOR

Coreen Turner has had a lifelong interest in literary houses, and Charlotte Brontë's home, Haworth Parsonage, was her first love. She enjoys going beyond the documentary evidence of biography to pursue what might have happened, and the surprising marriage of the most famous novelist of her age to her father's curate challenged her imagination. She is currently working on Mrs Dickens' Friend, *an exploration of the life of Julia Leigh Hunt who appears in this story. She lives in Stratford upon Avon.*

This story is based on real people and events.

'All the imagination needs is the stimulus of facts.'
– Barry Unsworth, *'Losing Nelson'*, 1999.

INTRODUCTION

William Smith Williams, 1800-1875

An unsung hero of nineteenth-century literature; not for him the blaze of Dickensian popularity or the huge financial deals that George Eliot achieved. He was that rare animal, an instinctive arbiter of quality and success when the manuscripts came thudding across his desk as he burned the candle late at the publishing house of Smith Elder. A shadowy but compelling figure, he knew writers as distant in time from each other as Leigh Hunt and Wilkie Collins, John Keats and Charlotte Brontë, even reaching a finger into the twentieth century with Leslie Stephen, father of Virginia Woolf.

His instinct for literature was matched by his desire to nurture the talents he served, accompanying the tubercular poet on his last journey and comforting the tubercular novelist in her north country fastness. He kept the hundreds of letters that Charlotte Brontë wrote to him as she endured her serial bereavements; he sent her books, reviews and magazines, and on her visits to London he entertained her in his home and endured her prickly social manner as she battered her way through literary London. Then suddenly, in 1853, she sacked him, without explanation, apology, or gratitude: she returned the books so regularly and kindly sent with a terse note: 'Do not trouble yourself to select or send any more books. These courtesies must cease some day - and I would rather give them up than wear them out.'

Just as suddenly, in 1854, she sent him her wedding card. What could have happened in between? Join him in middle age as he hurries through dark London streets to answer her summons.

CHAPTER 1

Mr Williams Meets a Train

1853

He hated the dawn. Hurrying through the silent streets he could not escape the tattered sleeping children, in doorways, in alleys, under carts, curled upon gratings, warm air fluttering their rags like tiny dying birds. When he hurried out of the theatres at night, clutching pencilled notes in his white kid-gloved hand, the flaring gaslight of the gin shops and dance halls cast a cosmetic vivacity on their thin faces. The little girls twirled in the golden light, absorbed in snatches of seductive music; but in their dawn sleep the angelic softness vanished as the cold pinched and their dreams recalled their violent lives.

He usually avoided the dawn by striking out east towards the newspaper offices immediately after the performance, a habit developed when he was younger and reviewed to relieve the dreariness of his employment as a publisher's bookkeeper. Then he had to get the copy in and still be at his desk early; no choice with eight children and a frail wife. His long stride had propelled him through the noisy crowds in the Haymarket, his clear intentions repelling the drunks and the women. Now that his finances were more secure he still kept the habit, frequently passing his friend Dickens as he hurried towards his own deadlines, his pleasure in walking long distances matching his obsession with the serial novel.

But today Williams had risen before the grey light had penetrated his terraced Kensington villa, and slipped quietly out without waking his sleeping family. Campden Hill was quiet, rural, beautiful, truly peaceful without the incessant clatter of hooves. He was a tall, greying man, surprisingly graceful in movement, his expression contemplative, absorbed. He covered the two miles to Euston in less than an hour. His Bradshaw had confirmed the arrival of the night train from Yorkshire at seven o'clock. She was not one to indulge the comfort of others, or even her own, so the earliness of her summons had not surprised him. The sleeping forms were more numerous as he approached the white Greek portico of the railway station; the vast open space in front of it was nightly host to prostitutes and beggars who preyed upon the new arrivals from the north of England. There was little protection for them from the winds that blew across the open fields beyond the station. What else could they do, he thought guiltily, but share in the opportunity of this great railway prosperity? But he held his pockets close as he scattered coins to ease his passage. The hooting and wailing, the shouts of guards, passengers clinging together, the lone beggar children who managed to elude all the rules of platform tickets to assail the new arrivals, made melancholy rise within him, and he tried the distraction of the bookstall of W. Henry Smith, his practised eye scanning for familiar names. Everyone read on the train now, even at night when the swaying oil lamps gave scanty illumination, and the canniest publishers had quickly flooded the Smith stalls with cheap books.

Feeling for his watch, he glanced at it and moved quickly towards the platform. He wanted to be there before her, to observe her demeanour, to try to read the purpose of her journey. As the locomotive heaved towards him in its last throes it enveloped the whole platform in hissing vapour; he strained his short-sighted eyes to see the doors opening, huddles of passengers moving towards him, obliterating those following behind. He stood still, searching the clearing horizon, his heart thudding as fewer and fewer passengers and porters remained. Perhaps she had changed her mind. The final lingering plumes cleared and revealed a tiny figure clutching a single bag, motionless, observing. He began what seemed an endless walk towards her. She didn't move, her head slightly inclined to focus better on the distance. Arriving, he daringly took her gloved hands in his and kissed them. She did not flinch.

'Mr Williams,' she murmured, the shy smile spreading to her fine grey eyes, 'you came!'

'Miss Brontë,' he replied, stooping low to hide his happy face, 'how could I stay away?'

'My tears are not for you,' she said as he attempted to guide her towards a cab, her handkerchief fluttering. 'I had a cinder in my eye, and it still bothers me.'

His task was made more difficult by her unceasing observation. Every passenger, beggar, prostitute, was swept meticulously by her sharp grey eyes. He almost fell over as she stopped suddenly at the Smith's bookstall.

'Mine?' she queried.

'Not yet,' he replied, 'but George is working on it.' A shadow passed over her face.

'Routledge has a good line in pulp for the railway, and Longman is reprinting Scott at a great rate. We have to find exactly the right place for you.'

She sighed and clung more tightly to his arm. 'Everything is difficult. Even getting to London. Do you know, a dear little girl deposited her previous breakfast in my lap on the way here! You may detect the event still.' She sniffed the air. 'I did what I could with handkerchief and water.'

The cab they climbed into was greasy and slightly rank in the way of all hackneys. 'You'll hardly notice in here,' he said, handing her in as the driver remained resolutely surly in his seat. They sat back in the lumpy upholstery, watching the sky redden; did he imagine it or was she leaning closer to him?

***

'It was so sudden,' he said. He held her hands, trying to lessen her distress. 'You know – love at first sight.'

She had disappeared on arrival in Bedford Square, and he had sat, alone and unoccupied, listening to the muffled sounds of the respectable boarding house, bracing himself for whatever was to come. Eventually the door opened softly and she came and sat beside him, subsiding in a whisper of silk, changed, neat and faintly smelling of lavender.

'Real love is not at first sight.' she replied sharply. 'Real love is born of mutual understanding of character, intellect, suffering…'

He held the tiny hands tighter. 'My dear Miss Brontë, surely it is true for some at first sight – remember Romeo and Juliet!'

She looked down. 'They were children,' she whispered, 'mere children. For mature people, passionate, intelligent people with judgement – it cannot be.' She was shaking.

Disturbed by the intensity of her feelings, he rose and crossed the room to the window where thick muslin absorbed the clatter of the horses passing in the Square. Outside the day was dismally normal: rain dripped from the trees in the gardens opposite, a few vendors' cries filtered through from Gower Street, the drumming of passing boots beat a faint tattoo. Inside, the room was a vortex of emotion.

'I'm sorry I wrote so sharply,' she said. She certainly knew how to disarm a man. He had always felt that her decision to send Jane Eyre away from Rochester's adulterous proposals had been a difficult one for such a sexually charged woman. The irregular teeth heightened her smile, brightened now by the tears which clung to her thick lashes. 'You didn't deserve that. You've been such a good friend since Branwell died, and then Emily and Anne…' She stopped and took some deep breaths. 'I couldn't bear the thought of losing George…' He passed her his handkerchief, more used to wiping sweat and ink than tears. 'I wrote even more sharply to him, you know.'

He did. George Smith, his employer at the publishers Smith Elder, who published *Jane Eyre* to a rapturous world, had shown him the letter.

'We have no secrets, Will,' he had said, fluttering the letter onto Williams's desk. 'At least not where the Brontës are concerned. This is how she congratulates me on my engagement! And I thought we were friends!'

Williams had swivelled in his seat to read, avoiding picking up so personal a correspondence:

In great happiness as in great grief - words of sympathy should be few. Accept my meed of congratulation. Sincerely yours, C Brontë.

He had looked up at his employer's handsome young face, the dark eyes puzzled, brow furrowed.

'Perhaps you mistook the nature of your friendship. You publish her works, are midwife to her children, as it were. You give her a life too. She loses a brother and two sisters. She's alone in a moorland village with her intelligent but elderly father. You are both young and unattached. You didn't see…?'

Smith had slumped into a chair, dark curls spilling into his rummaging hands. 'I didn't ask you for a synopsis of a novel. But I grant that you're the perceptive one. I'm the bookseller. You're the one with an eye for emotional content. But this isn't a story, Will!'

'No, but it seems she loved you and hoped for the

marriage of your souls as well as a successful business partnership. Even to a dispassionate observer like myself it seemed possible that you were attracted to her. She strikes out when she's hurt. Remember *Jane Eyre*?'

'I'm so sorry.' Smith rose and stretched his long body, prematurely stooped from the thirty-seven hour stints he often worked to pay off the debts created by his dishonest partner. Staring financial ruin in the face, with the prospect of losing the business, he had saved his widowed mother's fortune, as well as his sisters', after he had found the accounting falsifications. Ethical beyond his years, he had resolved to pay off every creditor as well as increase and maintain the publishing firm founded by his father. The bright necktie, awry from his long night's labours, was an odd contrast to his sober suit. 'I suppose it might have worked if I had not met my fiancée; but Miss Brontë of all people should know the inescapable nature of love. Try to smooth things over. Perhaps she'll write to you.'

She did.

Do not trouble yourself to select or send any more books. These courtesies must cease some day – and I would rather give them up than wear them out.

Ouch.

And then she came to London.

CHAPTER 2

Miss Brontë's Dilemma

'Papa,' she said, pleating the olive silk of her frock between her nervous fingers, 'Papa does not want me to marry Mr Nicholls.'

'And you? Do you want to marry him?'

She groaned faintly. 'I want to marry someone. I want to feel passion – again,' she blushed, 'and be free in someone else's soul.' She looked directly at him. 'It is possible, you know, I know it is possible. My parents, I think, were like that. My father married quite late but he was in love with my mother for the rest of his life. Still is.' She sniffed. 'She died over thirty years ago. He gave me her letters to read, letters he has kept all these years, the paper so thin from his re-reading.' She laughed suddenly. 'She called him her "saucy Pat". Can you imagine that?' She was on the verge of tears again. 'I want to love like that. I did with M Heger.' (*Snakes alive,* thought Williams, *the forbidden subject! The married man in Brussels!*) 'Foolishly I thought that Mr Smith – George – and I…' Her voice trailed away. Handkerchief time again.

He whispered: 'This Mr Nicholls; your father's curate?'

'Yes.'

'But curates…'

'I know, I know.' She sounded really cross. She took another deep breath and shuddered to stability. 'I know I have pilloried curates. I actually had two proposals from curates before Mr Nicholls. Emily used to berate me for the way I wrote about them – because she said I was denigrating Papa, who had been a curate. Of course I was not. But *Shirley* drew it all out of me and I can think more kindly now.' *How convenient*, thought Williams. 'So I must consider Mr Nicholls.'

Thick fog outside had turned the late morning into night. She pulled her shawl around her thin shoulders and went to the window to draw the curtains. The brass rings clunked into the thick velvet and she lit the two candles the landlady had left.

Williams considered his position. He was beginning to understand; and he was flattered. He smiled faintly. The greatest romantic novelist of the decade had come to London to seek his advice about love. Arranging his long body comfortably on the chaise longue, he smiled secretly, and waited. But he was wrong.

***

'I need to know,' she continued, perilously balancing her coffee cup, 'about marriage. Not love, I know about love.' She blushed and kept her eyes away from his. As the reader at Smith Elder he was familiar with the Brontë mix of reality and imagination. *Villette* had so disturbed George Smith that he had delayed its publication. Williams had been deeply moved by it. Yes, she certainly knew about love.

'It's marriage – I can't remember our parents' marriage – I was only six when Mama died. So despite the passion I know was between them, I never saw the daily living that people have to do. I've only observed it in the families where I was a governess.' She grimaced. 'Men are often absent – servants intervene and smooth the way. That's not what it would be for me and Mr Nicholls. But you – you surely know?'

He was transfixed by her face. She had always considered herself ugly, had caricatured her looks in *Jane Eyre;* she was tiny, with a head out of proportion to her body, but in this soft light she had a beauty he had not seen before. He could imagine how the yearning Nicholls would see her at the fireside in Haworth, the flames licking away the lines around her mouth, burnishing her beautiful eyes, her glossy hair unrestrained by a bonnet.

'Mr Williams?' Her voice recalled him, that tantalising mixture of Irish and Yorkshire. The girls at her school had said she had an Irish accent at fifteen, the indelible influence of her indomitable and devoted father. 'Will? I hope I am not improper to ask you such a question?' There was real anxiety in her voice.

He leant towards her, maintaining a respectable distance, his hands clasped between his knees, half a smile on his lips.

'No,' he said, 'I am just full of thoughts. You are

right to distinguish between love and marriage. You are right that I know about both.' He chuckled. 'When you visited my family you saw the fruits of love – eight children – and the state of the marriage. Your question is very interesting. Few women would pose it with such honesty. But then you are not as other women. Your writing has made you independent; you have money. It is your own, not family money; you can afford to choose.'

She sighed. 'All the money in the world will not make me less lonely. When Branwell, Emily, and Anne were alive I had no need of other people. We were perfect – oh, we had rows and frustrations and even odd jealousies to do with our writing, and a really bad falling out once, but we were always together. Even Branwell's problems with drink and laudanum, and the difficulties they made in our daily living, seemed to bind us together even closer. Now there is only me and Papa, and he cannot live much longer. People pity me for living with him in gloomy Haworth, but you have no idea what an interesting companion he is – old fashioned in some ways but ahead of his time in others. And so clever! He has been an inspiration to us all our lives. The books he has written were on the shelves and everything else open to us to read - Byron, Shakespeare...' Her voice trailed away. 'He had very humble beginnings in Ireland, managed to reach Cambridge when he was twenty-five, and did brilliantly, but when he goes I shall be completely alone, now I know that George doesn't want me. You're a very married man. I can't ask anyone else!'

He laughed unrestrainedly this time at this description. 'How accurate you are! Now I understand why you've come.' Daringly, he leaned forward and tucked a stray lock of hair behind her ear. She shook her head a little but smiled at him. 'I'll think about your problem. But tonight we will go to the opera and suspend disbelief. Tomorrow we will think seriously about marriage!'

CHAPTER 3

Tears at the Opera

Charlotte sat very still in front of the looking glass. It was a handsome piece, mahogany, polished, the glass clear and unspeckled, matching the fine heavy furniture which endorsed the respectability of the boarding house. In Haworth she rarely looked at her reflection; the only good looking glass was in her father's room, where he and Branwell shaved; she and her sisters piled up their hair in fragments of glass, only checking the even distribution of the style.

The candle flickered as a door banged on the landing, temporarily shadowing her face. She looked hard and long into her eyes, and dragged the fingers of each hand slowly down either side of her cheeks. The skin resettled itself, and she sat, hands in lap, still looking. Under her eyes were the dark patches of dehydration from the railway journey; like most women she avoided drinking on the train which had no conveniences. With what relief she had repaired to Mrs

Tait's mahogany seated, porcelain painted water closet, so new and daring. She was so thirsty she had drunk the entire contents of the water carafe placed by her bedside. Her complexion lacked the whiteness of pale London ladies, their parasols at the ready to bar the sun's rays. The moors behind her father's Parsonage had been playground to her and her siblings from their motherless early childhoods; Patrick Brontë was busy with the parish, their aunt huddled over a small fire in her room to combat the change from sunny to Cornwall to ferocious Yorkshire, pattens clicking on the stone floors to repel the damp. At least they could hear her coming. She smiled into the looking glass, and the wrinkles round her eyes fanned out. The ruddy cheeks, testament to years of sun, wind, and rain on the moors, dimpled back at her.

She had opted for a single bag for this journey to London. The station at Keighley was four miles on foot from Haworth, much of it through fields as a short cut: she had had no time to send a box on in advance and, however buoyant the mood at imminent escape, bags became heavy in the last stages. Her brush and comb, a tiny bottle of lavender water, and some handkerchiefs lay beside the looking glass, underclothes discreetly in the drawer below. Beside her bed lay a copy of *The Town,* by Leigh Hunt, sent to her recently by Mr Williams; next to that, pencil and paper to catch thoughts. In the wardrobe hung her other frock, the travelling one, grey, serviceable, now brushed from the journey and ready to wear again, ready for a clean collar. She looked at the grey frock and decided it was not for the opera tonight. What would Mr Williams like her to wear? As if he cared. She shrugged. Tonight she had not only to go to the opera but face George Smith, and possibly his new fiancée; she felt utterly foolish but completely determined to overcome the situation. She'd sparkle if she could, but play the serious lady novelist if she could not. *Come on,* she thought, *just get on with it.*

She brushed her hair energetically, the brush slapping and slithering down its length, noting anxiously the thinning crown, then, parting it and coiling it into a neat bun, she stood straight and looked at her reflection. She wondered what her mother would have looked like. She'd seen portraits, but the whole body, the *bella figura*? Papa was tall, still had the clothes he wore at Cambridge copied by the Haworth tailor, so little had his figure changed. But she was small, and yes, neat, perhaps more like her mother. She straightened herself, then bent to remove a burr and a leaf from the hem of her cloak as she put it on, and went down to the sitting room.

Williams arrived within five minutes. He had suggested a cab but she had told him she wanted to walk to Covent Garden after sitting all night in the train. She loved the lights and noise and bustle. At this time in Haworth just one cheap candle would glimmer from cottages whose occupants could afford to light them; the rest would be in bed in retreat from the darkness. At the back of the Parsonage on nights when there was no moon, there was total blackness, nothing until the light glimmered faintly in the dawn and slipped through the Parsonage curtains. In these London streets there was a danger, a thrill in the flaring torches, clattering horses and the glimpses into the gorgeously bright shops – still open! – and chophouses and pubs. The town's perilous energy thrilled her, and she enjoyed leaning on Williams, feeling his warmth and strength, his protection.

Sometimes she had to skip to keep up with his long stride, but she was quick and nimble. He looked down at her animated face, framed in her silk ruched bonnet, and smiled.

'All right?'

'Most certainly!'

But as they got nearer to the Opera House he felt her gripping tensely on his arm. He put his hand over hers, knowing that she was anticipating the meeting with George Smith, dreading appearing to be the spurned woman in front of his new fiancée, Elizabeth Blakeway. He took a chance.

'She probably has no idea that you hoped for George; he's a gentleman and would not have told her even if he realised. There has been no gossip.'

She blushed. 'Really? I thought that was too much to expect. Then I'll just face him as if it had never occurred to me that he would make a good husband as well as publisher!'

'Good girl. Come on, I said we'd meet them in our seats.'

They pushed through crowds to the facade of the Opera House. Beggars hovered, seizing every opportunity before they were pushed away by the theatre staff, used to complaints from the punters. Charlotte hated this part of street life, aware that very fine lines divide the warm and fed from the cold and starving. On her father's death, she would have to leave the Parsonage. Without the success of her writing, she and her siblings, had they lived, would have been forced back to being governesses and tutors, servants sheltering in the houses of ridiculous moneyed people with badly behaved children, until they either died young or went to the Workhouse. A shiver passed through her. Without her books, she too might be whining at the doors of the Opera House.

'Give me your cloak.' It was Williams, easing her path again. She attempted a bright smile, handing him the cloak and bonnet which he passed to the stewardess. She raised a hand to settle her hair, tucked in a curl, then smoothed her dress. The olive silk was just right. The red interior of the Opera House, lit by bright chandeliers which swayed as the doors swung open and shut again, smelt of wax, cigar smoke, and wine with an undertow of sweat, dust, and damp. Swishing along behind him, they arrived in the Circle. George Smith, upright, handsome, dark, charming, was waiting.

She took a deep breath before he spotted them.

'George,' said Williams. 'Here we are. Miss Brontë insisted on walking. She's very fit.' George bowed and kissed her hand.

'Delighted to see you so unexpectedly, Miss Brontë,' he said. 'And what an opportunity – may I present my fiancée, Miss Blakeway?'

Charlotte went into novelist mode. She raised her head and fixed Miss Blakeway with a kindly quizzical air, but before she could speak, the girl said, in a rush, 'I'm so pleased to meet you, Miss Brontë! I love your novels, I've read every one. I've told George he's so lucky to know you. I knew I would meet you one day.

I've looked forward to this so much.'

Charlotte was disarmed. She was a beautiful, charming girl. Of course George would love her the moment he saw her. 'I have heard so much about you,' she said softly. 'Mr Smith is indeed lucky to have you.' She felt an odd sense of relief. Seeing them together somehow lifted a burden from her. He was a charmer, but perhaps just a good business man. No soulmate. She saw Williams looking at her. Thankfully she moved towards to him.

'Well done,' he whispered. 'Come and sit by me.'

'She really is a – stunner? Is that the new word?' breathed Charlotte back.

'Yes, that's what the painters say these days, and she is remarkably good looking, a classical face. But without the beauty of thought and genius in it,' he said playfully. She subsided into the seat beside him in a rustle of silk. Her face expressed confusion. Had she really heard that?

The Marriage of Figaro began and gradually the noisy audience came under its spell. Charlotte looked round without moving and wondered how many of them had come for the music and how many to see and be seen. Glancing at George along the row, she speculated on his motive: had he come for the music or had his ethical but commercial soul been prompted by the literary contacts he might make? Williams was looking at her as if he read her calculations; she tried to moderate her thoughts by thinking of the number of her novels which had been bought merely to enhance a drawing room sofa table. Suddenly, the orchestral mood changed: they had reached the Countess's lament, the music gently pulsing beneath the exquisitely rising melody. It caught her unawares; suddenly tears were spilling down her cheeks. A handkerchief was pushed into her hand. Williams turned to her as she groped for it and she could see tears standing in his eyes. When her vision cleared she looked at George. He was dry-eyed; fiddling with his programme.

Outside a steady rain had started to fall and without consultation Williams hailed a cab. Neither of them spoke; the regular jolting was calming, the carriage lamps throwing intermittent light on their faces in time to the horses' hooves. Williams hummed the last bars of the countess's aria; Charlotte sighed. He put his hand over hers and looked out at the shining wet streets. She, rarely lost for words, was speechless, made dumb by the intensity of her feelings.

The horse's gait slowed as the cabby drew level with her boarding house. Williams climbed out and stood on the pavement, his arm extended to hand her down, rain gathering on his black coat as she hesitated and gathered her skirts. Standing beneath him she raised her face but found no words of thanks coming. In a moment of rare impetuosity he bent and gently kissed her hair where it protruded from her bonnet, then equally quickly propelled her up the steps and into the hallway, closing the door behind her. He paid the waiting cab, tipping generously as he did not want to retain it. He wanted to walk; and he needed to think.

CHAPTER 4

Enter Mr Keats

The next day was like another country. Clear blue skies, frost which whitened the trees and shrubs in the gardens opposite her boarding house. He, who had passed a wakeful night in his chilly marital bed, raised the handsome brass knocker of her door just as Mrs Tait opened it. 'The young lady is in her sitting room, sir,' she said pleasantly. There was no hint of criticism of him, an older man visiting a younger woman without chaperone. *Perhaps impropriety is unbelievable,* he thought wryly, *my age and her demeanour.* She, who had lain awake most of the night appalled at the intensity of her emotions, was pretending to read.

'I thought you weren't coming!' she said, springing up to greet him. There was an informality about her which he had never seen before. 'I thought you might have decided my questions were foolish. And the opera—'

Following his instincts, he put his fingers to her

lips. 'I have thought of little else and I have the answer,' he murmured. 'Get your cloak and bonnet. On a day such as this we shall walk in the gardens and you can think about your decisions.'

Later, her arm tucked unprotestingly and tightly into his, he said, 'How much do you know about me?'

'Everything,' she replied. 'I have known you since you told George he must publish *Jane Eyre* – I have written hundreds of letters to you, and received as many in reply. There is little I cannot know about you.'

'That is my very recent past,' he replied, slashing a few innocent branches with his umbrella. 'But the rest of my life is an excellent canvas from which you can learn about marriage and love, and I insist you include love. When I was seventeen I worked for the publishers Taylor and Hessey, and I knew Keats. I worked with Hazlitt, John Clare, and Leigh Hunt. I have lived next door to George Henry Lewes, and with Thornton Hunt. I know Thackeray and Carlyle. These connections have stayed with me all my life.'

She stopped walking, and finding a bench to sit on looked at him in amazement. 'You never told me any of this!'

'You never asked. Most of our relationship has been to do with your writing and the very great tragedies in your family. I was grateful to smooth your path a little. Admiring creative people has been at the heart of my life, a great consolation to me.' He looked embarrassed. 'When I met Keats we were both young men, he hugely talented.' His blue eyes held hers. 'You can have no idea what it is to see blazing talent, and suddenly know you yourself have none. Miss Brontë…'

'Charlotte.'

'Charlotte.' He paused, relishing it. 'Charlotte. I wanted to write poetry, and thought my apprenticeship at Taylor's was the path to it. But when I met Keats I knew I was simply in the shadow of his burning sun. It was a very hard lesson for a young man to learn. But eventually I realised I could serve the talent of others, and when I met you another talent blazed for me.'

'It doesn't feel like that, Mr Williams.'

'Will.'

'Will. It doesn't, Will. Nothing blazes. Sometimes I write more quickly than at other times. It's a hard labour with finishing the greatest pleasure.'

He drew her to her feet and they walked in silence between the glistening trees. There were no other walkers that day. A single brave bird poured out its song above them.

'My point is,' he said hesitantly. Ever since she had known him Charlotte had been surprised by his hesitant delivery, so utterly different from the firm fluency of his letters. 'My point is that long observation of the lives and loves of talented people makes me especially suited to advise on your… problem. Your talent gives you the same needs in love and marriage as these people. Where do you want to start? I can show requited love, pure passion, lust, forbearance…'

'Let's start with pure passion,' she said without hesitation. 'I grant the need to include love as we consider marriage. But pure passion is not what I have for Mr Nicholls, that's more Emily's Cathy and Heathcliff. But I want to know about it. Who will it be?'

'Keats, of course,' he smiled, 'and the poor bewildered Fanny Brawne.'

She stood back from him a little; she loved his smile, his strong white teeth and the way his plain black clothes defined his still handsome face and grey hair. 'What excitement!' she said, a bright spot glowing on her cheek. 'Give. I never thought I'd know someone who knew Keats!'

CHAPTER 5

Young Mr Williams

1820

He had been flicking ink pellets into the coal scuttle for about half an hour, enjoying their parabolic progress through the shaft of weak sunlight which started at the shop door's fanlight and ended on the paper-strewn floor.

'Scuse me *if* you don't mind, Mr Williams,' growled Benyon the porter, viciously removing the coal scuttle so that the final pellet smacked the wall and sprayed it, '*if* you don't mind me interrupting your *work*.' He rolled his arthritic hip towards the back door, muttering curses as he went, ending them with a slam which rocked the building. Williams blushed. That was the way at Taylor and Hessey, most of the time working every hour God sent, then lulls when you were too tired to think.

When he had come as an apprentice he had not really understood the arrangements for his pay – seventeen and six a week with dinner, hours nine to eight except at magazine time, lodgings above the shop. Magazine time extended to whenever deadlines were tight, and then he and everyone else worked through the night.

Apart from Benyon, he was the lowliest employee except the cat, who worked for its living mousing to protect the piles of printed paper, the books and magazines which were stacked on every available surface. That morning James Hessey had descended from his home above the shop at 93 Fleet Street to find the newly printed edition of John Clare's *Poems* narrowly escaped from the nibbling which had severely damaged the umpteenth edition of Mrs Taylor's *Practical Hints for Young Females*, Taylor and Hessey's most essential pot-boiler. Husky, a magnificent tabby with a fine white face and regal aspect, imported from Hessey's parents' home in Yorkshire, worked strict hours and only at night. By day he followed the sun round the shop, gravitating to the parlour fire when it disappeared towards the west in the afternoon.

Williams worked much harder. There was nothing he would rather do than be in this shop with the books, his employers, and most of all, the poets and writers who were in and out all day and often well into the night. He worked long hours making clean copies of the works for publication for the printers, his rapid, clear handwriting fluently covering page after page, his eyes and head aching at night as he checked every word, and then checked again. As the nights wore on his curly blond hair darkened with sweat. He now came in well before nine to get daylight hours for his work, fearing errors in his copy from candle light.

'Will you change the meaning of my work, young Will?' John Keats had said, laughing, scanning the page Williams had just finished. 'Perhaps you know better but if you don't mind I would love to keep my comma there!'

Williams's ready blush had suffused his fair skin. He loved Keats and would not for world have allowed an error in his copy. Of all the writers who dropped in and out of the shop and parlour he worshipped the small vibrant poet, whose vivid face and burning eyes encapsulated everything that Williams wanted a poet to be, the pugnacious mouth belying the gentle nature. Keats's singular style of dress, his collar open, neckerchief tied untidily, symbol of his liberal, Byronic following, became Williams' style too, until John Taylor, looking up from his latest cryptogram to sign a letter Will had written for him, observed dryly:

'This is excellent work, Will, but you will wear a stock to work. Genius may break the rules. You and I may not, while we work here.' He must have noted the smallest defiance lurking on his young employee's face, for he added more kindly, 'Will, it is hard for us not to think we are as the writers we publish. When I first started this business I suppose I hoped that I would end up writing for a living, not printing and publishing and selling stationery to make ends meet. But I know that I have not the smallest talent compared with the writers we serve. That is why I spend my time trying to solve my cryptograms, it requires patience and a reasonable critical faculty which I know I have. I do not have imagination and genius. Neither, I suspect, do you.'

The friendly grey eyes, deeply set beside a long, strong nose, scrutinised Williams. Taylor was a bachelor, dedicated to the work of his writers. He, like his friend and partner James Hessey, had come adventuring from the country, meeting when both were apprentices in the Temple of the Muses, a gorgeous, pretentious bookshop in Finsbury Square, whose flamboyant appearance contrasted strangely with the skinflint pay the young men received. They were soon running their own booksellers, adding pens, ink, paper, pencils, account books, ledgers, bill books, pocket books, commonplace books, every writing trifle to keep in profit in the early years. Hessey was musical, was a lively dancer, had a good baritone and was a competent flautist; popular in drawing rooms, he was soon married and raising his young family above the shop in Fleet Street. Taylor, shyer, more intense, moved out to lodgings. They were complementary; Hessey handled the business and Taylor the authors, always in agreement on policy and editing. Taylor treated his apprentices like sons, encouraging them to use their leisure time well, to learn French and Greek, as he had done, to listen to what was going on around them. Williams had been avoiding the clear gaze, but now looked up and said, 'I know. You're right. I'm quite jealous of Keats's talent. My clothes,' he tugged embarrassedly at his loosely tied white neckerchief, 'are the closest I will get to it.'

Taylor steepled his fine, thin fingers and leaned back in his chair. 'I know,' he said gently, 'I am sure that for poetic genius there is not Keats equal living. But you have learned your lesson young. It will free you to be the midwife to their work. Their works are like children to them – the conception, the growth, the birth, and then having to live with the consequences of passion when the reviews come in.'

'How can they be so cruel to Keats?' Williams burst out vehemently. 'The *Quarterly*, and that joke of a magazine *Blackwoods* – how can they presume to criticise a genius—'

'It is part of the game,' interrupted Taylor, 'part of the business of writing. I know the reviews of *Lamia* and the other poems are better. There are a hundred and twenty copies ordered in advance – and one of them is for Mr Shelley.' His eyes twinkled. 'Mrs Gisborne will take it to Italy to him. That will cheer him. Go to Keats tomorrow and tell him this – he likes you and he needs help – these are simple things which will smooth his way. I've decided that whatever happens I'll fund him through his work, and I also want to send him to Italy, to the sun, to see if he can be cured. I will find the money to do this whatever happens. That is my link with genius – yours for the time being will be more active.' He stood up from his desk and went to the window where the traffic in Fleet Street clattered and rolled. The day was drawing in and the yellow city light made ochre shadows across the street. He drew the curtain and scattered some more coal over the dying embers of the fire. 'You can go to Hampstead tomorrow and talk to him about Italy. Try to persuade him to go. It is his only hope. There is nothing else we can do.'

Tears filled Will's eyes. His brushed his sleeve over his face and swallowed hard. Taylor turned and put his arm around his shoulders.

'Go to him tomorrow,' he repeated. 'You'll feel better if you are doing something positive to help him.

***

The night before, Williams had been tucked into the window seat in the parlour, his knees drawn up, chin resting, leaning against the bowing window. Outside in Fleet Street he knew the gaiety of the night was beginning; he could feel in his shoulder the vibrations of the carriages as they rolled towards Covent Garden and the theatres and entertainments that Taylor warned him against, as he had instructed him to keep away from the pornographers' shops in the little streets to the north of the Strand, when he did his printers' errands. Despite his youth Will had little inclination for either of these, being far more interested in the firm and its people who had become a family to him. His own parents were dead and his siblings scattered, apprenticed or married, whatever kept body and soul together. He wanted to be here, with Keats, observing, near to him. He had returned with the mutton chops and the coffee, which Taylor insisted were fetched to mop up Keats's claret and the brandy and water they all craved. After he had delivered them he looked towards the window seat and Taylor nodded. He knew the young man's worship of Keats and could see no harm in him staying, provided he was ready for work in the morning. The panelled room was hot. Keats too.

'He is so pompous!' he cried suddenly, thumping his fist on the table. 'Everything you send him he sends it back with an essay in poetical criticism! When I tried to argue a point with him, Mrs Wordsworth stopped me.' He rose from the table and minced over to Will, leaning forward, a hand delicately on his arm. '"Mr Wordsworth is never interrupted,"' he squeaked, falsetto, '"never interrupted!"' His handsome, good-natured face was momentarily angry, flushed to his temples. 'I know my limits but...'

Taylor stopped him. 'You don't have limits, John. Never think that!'

'But Wordsworth has, as you put it, the full blaze,' said Keats quietly. Claret usually made him sleepy, the reason for his overnight sojourns with his publishers. 'He thinks we need taking down a peg – do you remember when I read him *Endymion* and he said, "A very pretty piece of Paganism"? It is odd that being one of us he misjudges our need for warmth.' As if to emphasise his point he spread his hands before the blazing fire. 'We need warmth and wine and love and praise – and here we get it,' he said, indicating John Taylor. He clambered onto a chair, his small stature leaving him room to raise his glass high. 'To Taylor – and Hessey – the sweetest publishers a poet ever had.' He sat down. Taylor rose and bowed.

Taylor had been as excited as Williams when the copies of *Lamia* arrived. Benyon had pushed them on his ancient worm-eaten sack barrow from the printers in Cornhill, taking his time as he gossiped to his friends about the goings on of poets and publishers, easing his brown paper parcels onto the floor of the shop as slowly as he could, eyeing Williams all the time to prevent him having the huge pleasure of unwrapping the new volumes.

'*My* job, Mr Williams,' he said pompously, untying the complicated knots very slowly, '*my* job to fetch from the printers and deliver unwrapped and untouched to Mr Taylor or Mr Hessey, who if I am not mistaken are both out till later…'

'I'm here, Benyon,' said Taylor, emerging from the parlour, his clothes crumpled from the night before, waiting for just this moment. He himself could have waited quite happily asleep at his lodgings in New Bond Street. Behind him Keats lolled against the door jamb, his poet's neckerchief nicely matching the black eye he sported where a cricket ball had hit him as he and Taylor whiled away the hours till morning.

'Right, then, sir,' said Benyon, even more officiously, 'I will hand the merchandise to you and then it is not my—'

'Merchandise!' cried Keats, nearly knocking him down as he sprinted towards the books. 'Them's not merchandise, them's me poems, Benyon. Poems!' He picked up a volume and raised it to the light, the gold lettering on the spine catching the early morning sun. He kissed it gently, turning it over in his hands, breathing deeply to smell the new binding and uncut paper. Suddenly, he staggered and fell onto the stool at William's desk, his arms spread-eagled to support him, consumed by a spasm of coughing.

Hessey waited for him to breathe freely again and led him back into the parlour. Settling him in a chair, he said quietly, 'Stay calm, John, or you'll take away all the pleasure you have in the new book.' Keats smiled wryly, covering his mouth with a handkerchief which flooded red as he held it there.

'I am enough of a doctor to know arterial blood when I see it,' he panted, referring to his training at St Thomas's Hospital, when the coughing subsided. 'A doctor will do little good.' His chest heaved as he lay back exhausted. Taylor summoned Williams with a nod.

'Go for Doctor Darling,' he said quietly, 'there's a terrible fever on him. Tell him to come quickly.' Williams was at the door before he had finished.

CHAPTER 6

Keats in Love

He scattered sand across his last letter and put it on the partners' desk that Taylor and Hessey shared. He wasn't quite sure what to take to Hampstead besides the extra copies of *Lamia* – should he take a bottle of claret, or would one of Keats's friends have done this? Might it appear presumptuous for a mere clerk to take such a gift to a writer? He desperately wanted this visit to go well, although it would tax his inexperience. But Taylor had not chosen him for his experience. He had chosen him because he knew the young man's heart was entirely given to the young poet, that his affection made him incapable of a misplaced word. He had noticed early a rare sensitivity in Williams, both to literature and to the writers who brought their work to the firm; it was as if he knew instinctively about the wrestle with words, the loneliness, the stamina required; and then his sympathy was palpable when they sat late in the parlour, elated or distressed by the reviewers. If anyone could persuade Keats to go to

Italy he felt Williams could. His youth helped him to understand the main obstacle better than most.

It was midday when Williams started, walking swiftly out of the dusty city, buying a pie from one of the numerous shops that sold them to the workers who arrived hungry from long walks from villages and fortified themselves before starting the long walk back. He soon left behind the noise and crowds as he took the back lanes which he knew well from having been sent on errands to Leigh Hunt's cottage in the Vale of Health; Hunt had now moved to Camden Town and Keats had lived with him through his long illness, kindly cared for, but suffering greatly from the chaos of the household, its many undisciplined children, and the volatile Mrs Hunt. Now he was living at Wentworth Place.

The journey through the lanes delighted him, the tall grasses were fragrant in the sun and the poppies and campion scattered among them started lines running through his head. He stopped. *No more bad poetry*, he thought as he stripped a flowering grass between thumb and forefinger. *I know now what is good and what is bad, and Keats is good and Williams is pretty awful.* He smiled; his ability to spot a good writer compensated him for his own lack of poetic talent. He swung on, keeping beneath the shade of the ancient trees in the afternoon heat. It was through these lanes that the poets walked when they had visited Leigh Hunt; Coleridge and Keats and Charles Lamb, even Byron and Shelley had visited Hunt here in Hampstead. Williams shivered despite the heat of the day. He knew Keats lived about half a mile from Flask Walk, sharing a house with Charles Brown which was next to the

Brawne family. He had overheard Taylor and Hessey on the subject of the Brawnes, deprecating the daughter and the heartbreak she apparently caused Keats.

When he was a few yards from where he thought the house would be, Williams sat down in the shade of a massive oak, and tried to cool down. He took a clean stock out of his leather satchel and wound it round his neck, in deference to Taylor. He brushed down his clothes and removed the dust from his boots in the long grass. He had never seen the house before and was surprised, when he turned in at the gate, to see only one quite new square house surrounded by a garden. He let himself in quietly, shutting the gate carefully, for he could see that someone was sitting beneath a tree. As he got nearer, his heart started to thump. It was Keats, and he had to approach him from behind; he was unsure how to make his presence known. After standing behind the chair for a few seconds, he stepped forward and said, 'I have come from Mr Taylor, sir.'

Keats looked up. His face was slack with sadness; he blinked as if to banish it, and said slowly, 'Less of the sir, Will. You can call me John. God knows you have done enough for me in these last two years.' Will hoped he would not blush but felt the colour rising in his face. 'Don't shake your golden curls, Will, or you will start me off on another Greek poem. It's true; you have made sense of my manuscripts—'

'There was little to make sense of,' breathed Williams. 'Your writing is clear, the sense immediate—'

'But the pages are not always in order and there are the really, really long bits, the bits the *Quarterly* described as—'

'You should ignore them!' burst out Williams. 'When I read your *Chapman's Homer* I felt as you felt – I knew what poetry really was, and I knew that I would never write a line worthy of you. You have the power to—'

'I have no power, Will. Look at me – a wreck of a man like my brother, a doctor trained at St Thomas's who can't heal himself, a poet who will never be remembered because he died before he could write his best works.'

'That is not true.' Williams was gaining confidence. 'If you wrote nothing more the world would remember forever the *Nightingale, St Agnes,* the sonnets.' He stopped because he did not want to continue the theme of not writing any more.

'But will I be remembered after I die? Don't stand to attention, Will, sit here on the ground by me. The grass is dry and the scent of the flowers will send you to sleep.' He breathed deeply, as if to energise himself with the scents, then coughed a dry, hollow cough. Suddenly his body stiffened. In the distance, on the doorstep of the house, raised a little above them, a woman stood.

'That's my Fanny, my darling girl,' he whispered, laying a hand on Williams' arm to prevent him rising. 'Just sit, and look at her. Isn't she beautiful?' He pulled himself up slightly to see her better.

Williams looked. The young woman was looking across the garden, not in their direction but he could see her plainly. Younger than he was, she had a maturity in her pose which was almost alarming. Her dark hair was coiled high above her pale face, but

Williams did not see beauty; he felt a pang of disappointment that she should be less than perfect to cause such havoc in the poet's life. He glanced covertly at Keats and saw hopelessness in his face. At that moment a man came out from the house and paused on the steps. He was taller, and looked down on her, drew close to her, speaking to her, waiting for her laughter. He stood a minute longer and then went out of the garden.

Keats' face darkened.

'I can hardly bear to see her speak to another man. Brown is a great one for flesh and conquests – our maid Abigail is pregnant by him, and he is always on the town.' His face contorted, then relaxed. 'He is a good friend, and I should trust him. But when I cannot even follow them if they take a walk in the garden… and sometimes she goes out in town on her own, and she is engaged to *me*.' He started coughing again, this time he needed a handkerchief to take the bloody phlegm. 'It's because I shall die, and can never possess her, and I don't trust her, because she has a lively soul and I know she will want someone else.' He stopped, and Williams could see tears in his eyes.

He seized his chance. 'It needn't happen, it really needn't. If you get better, as you will if you go for the winter to a warm climate, you will return to be with Miss Brawne again.' He wanted to believe it himself.

Keats looked him full in the face. 'It is so incredibly kind of them all to want to send me to Italy. No man has ever had a publisher like Taylor. He has even borrowed money himself to help me, for these are lean times for him as for the rest of us… But they forget that I was five years an apothecary and a year a surgeon. I've seen consumption take my brother. I nursed him and lived with him – it is impossible that I do not have the disease from that, even if I did not know arterial blood when I see it on my linen.' He waved the red-spattered handkerchief like a battle flag. 'I cannot have my love, and I shall lose my life. But I shall never cease to love her, wherever I go.'

Cloud had taken away the brightness of the sun. Fanny turned and went into the house. Williams sat in silence; instinctively he knew that now was not the time to speak. He looked toward the rising ground beyond the house – it could have been here that Keats had written his *Ode to a Nightingale*, it fitted so perfectly. There was birdsong all around them, piercing and beautiful, full throated and passionate. He clasped his hands around his knees, and without looking at Keats, said, 'I know how it seems. But there must be hope while you live. Your talent is so great that I believe that you are here to forge a new era in English poetry. To prolong the use of that talent is your duty. To go to Italy is to proclaim your belief in your talent. We all believe in it – why not you?'

'Did some kind god send you to Taylor's, Will? Or bring me to that most gentle and kind publisher? I don't deserve the care you both show. But I need it. I need…' He stopped. Fanny Brawne came out of the house again and into the garden, stepping lightly on the springy grass to where the two men sat.

'Who is this, John?' When she smiled her broad full mouth curved back to show perfect teeth. Her blue eyes were bright, startling, mirrored in the matching watered silk of her dress.

'This, Fanny, is the kindest messenger a kind

publisher ever sent. Mr William Smith Williams of Taylor and Hessey. He has brought me more copies of *Lamia*.' Williams spread the slim volumes on top of his leather bag, carefully shielding them from the grass. Fanny bent and picked one up.

'That's nice, John, very nice.' Williams gulped. 'It's very nice.' She let the pages open and fall away from the spine. 'Shall I have one? I would indeed love to have one.'

Nice, thought Williams. He lay back in the grass, shielding his eyes in case his contempt for her showed. Keats was murmuring to her. Williams rolled over, lay on his chest as if he could not hear.

'Of course you shall, my darling girl,' Keats was saying. 'Take it now and I will write in it later.' She drifted away elegantly across the garden, her arms dropped at her side, the little volume swinging in her right hand. There was silence. Williams knew not to break it.

'Don't be too hard on her, Will,' said Keats, his voice low. 'She is but nineteen, and does not know the way of poetry. I love her for herself, not for her love of my poetry.' He sighed and closed his eyes, leaning back in the chair, his face towards the returning sun. 'The warmth feels healing. Perhaps I will go to Italy; but if I go, I'll lose her.'

Amen to that, thought Williams. Aloud he said, 'True love will wait. She will be here for your return.'

'My return? What an optimist you are. Here, help me back to the house. I can't get back on my own and Brown is out. I hardly want the Brawnes to see me in this state. If you will support me I shall look almost well.'

Williams put his arm around him and was appalled by the thin body he felt through the baggy clothes. A spasm of coughing started the moment they moved and he felt the brittle frame would shatter. Slowly they made their way to the house and slowly, very slowly climbed the steps and reached the drawing room Keats shared with Brown. He was completely exhausted and let Williams lower him gently onto the couch and fetch water. His breathing was like a dying dog's. Williams went back to the garden, tactfully allowing him to recover on his own. He divined that pouring with sweat and with his lungs spewing blood and phlegm was not how Keats wished to be seen. He picked up the volumes of *Lamia* and the papers near them. The sight of the familiar, good-tempered, garlanded handwriting made his eyes sting. Pausing, he listened before he re-entered the room, placing the papers and books on a table near the window, sitting down, appearing to be admiring the drawings on the wall.

'Tell Taylor I will go to Italy.' The voice from the other side of the room was soft, controlled. Coughing took the next sentence, but it was enough. Williams found the linen he needed; he wiped the wide mouth, smoothing the wet curls away from his face, looking into the too-bright eyes. *I will remember this as long as I live*, he thought.

'I will tell Mr Taylor the moment I get back,' he said quietly. 'He's already been checking on passages. Soon you will be on your way to warmth and healing.' Keats shook his head.

'On my way, Will, certainly. I shall miss you. Will Taylor not send you with me? You're too useful to him, there's faint hope of that.' Williams' hands trembled on the decanter; he had to steady them to stop the clinking of glass on glass. Carefully he poured the water and set it by the poet's elbow. He had already heard the planning. He chose his words, deliberately smiling.

'They have a much better companion planned for you. I think Mr Severn will go with you.'

Keats nodded.

'My friends make me believe in the holiness of the heart's affections,' he murmured. His eyes were closing, his breathing quiet but rapid. Williams waited until he was sure he was asleep, then shut the door softly behind him.

***

His journey back to Fleet Street took him twice as long. The warm night was soft and the trees hung about him like a green room, but his heart was heavy. He had believed that Italy would be a cure; now he knew it was but a faint chance. From time to time he lay down in the long grasses, wrestling with anger and grief. As he neared the city he wiped tears and sweat from his face, the extreme rosiness of his fair complexion defying his despair. The bustle of the city, usually a stimulus and excitement, was abrasive. Reaching the shop, he found Taylor in the parlour hunched over a cryptogram. Without waiting to be asked Williams slumped in a chair.

'He'll go,' he said wearily, 'but he is so tortured by love, or the need to be in love, that the longing will kill him.'

He closed his eyes. Taylor went to the dresser and poured a glass of claret. An undemonstrative man, this was the most he could do for his suffering apprentice. He poured one for himself, as an act of sympathy. Together they sat, in silence only broken by the ticking of the clock and the faint rumble of Fleet Street beyond the shutters, until Benyon shattered their collusion with the replenished coal scuttle for his eternal fires.

Taylor had found that the *Maria Crowther* departed from Gravesend in the middle of September. He booked two berths, even before he had persuaded Joseph Severn to go with Keats. Not that he needed much persuasion: the young painter, a recent winner of the Gold Medal at the Royal Academy, was keen to go for the opportunity to fill his eyes with Italian light and subjects for his painting. He also loved Keats and would have gone to a grave if required. Taylor had at first been concerned that he was too immature to take on the responsibility of the sick poet in a strange land; neither of them had been abroad, and although Shelley promised support and hospitality, it would be some time before they reached him in his villa on the coast. Williams watched the preparations covertly, his heart thudding when each new arrangement was made, the baggage, the carriage, the farewell preparation. Suddenly Taylor appeared by his desk.

'You'll have to go to Hampstead, Will, and bring him to us. Leigh Hunt will take him to the coach stop in Pond Street, but he'll have bags which he can't possibly be left to manage alone.'

The next Wednesday he walked the distance to Pond Street while it was cool. He had been awake half the night worrying how he would manage this most delicate of situations, a dying man saying goodbye to a girl he loved passionately. When he arrived Hunt was already there with Keats, managing the bags, keeping a cheerful chatter going. He had walked with the two lovers from the house as Brown was on his annual holiday in Scotland. *Whatever they say of Leigh Hunt,* thought Williams, *this is what he does really well, this unconditional friendship, this support of talent. I could well learn from him.* Fanny stood, pretty but remote, hands torturing a handkerchief. Fired at the thought of the damage this might do to Keats, he immediately followed Hunt's lead and became gregarious.

'Such a smart cap!' he cried, gently touching the embroidered travelling cap Keats wore. He tugged playfully at the beautiful brown curls which lay on his thin shoulders. Keats smiled faintly.

'Fanny has re-lined it for me, against the cold.' Williams tried for a subject less emotional. At that moment the rumbling of coach wheels could be heard and a team of horses clattered to a halt.

'Goodbye, John,' said Hunt, bending from his great height to envelope Keats in a hug. 'All will be well – you'll see, all will be well.' Keats' eyes were wet and he clung on to his friend.

'You've been so good to me, and I… have often been churlish.'

'No,' said Hunt, 'it's all been privilege and pleasure to me and Mrs Hunt.'

'Poor Mrs Hunt,' sighed Keats, 'I've sorely tried her.'

'She doesn't mind!' Hunt's tones were warm. 'Come Fanny, take your leave,' and he drew the girl towards the poet, who clung to her, then stepped back, shaking his head.

'My dearest girl,' he muttered huskily, 'my own, my dearest girl.' She held his hands tightly, and kissed him on the cheek. His forehead was beaded with sweat despite the cool day.

'I'll be here when you return, John,' she said softly. 'Get better and return to me.' She unfolded her balled handkerchief and wiped his brow. 'Get in the coach now.' Something in the scene had mesmerised the coachman. Instead of berating his passengers to get aboard and speed the journey, he was watching the pair, his reins slack in his hands. Suddenly a horse shook its head and the jingling roused him.

'Take the bag inside with you, sir,' he said to Williams, 'there's plenty of room.' Williams helped Keats into the coach and turned away from the final farewell. He heard the coachman speak to his horses.

'Walk on, walk on,' he said, and as if to himself, 'That's a sad sight!'

Fanny waved the coach out of sight, a diminishing figure in the morning mist. When she returned to Wentworth Place she wrote in her commonplace book: *Mr Keats left Hampstead.*

CHAPTER 7

Bright Star Eclipsed

The tide and weather controlled the departure of the *Maria Crowther* and it was not until the Sunday that word came that the tides were right. During these days little work was done in the shop or parlour which hummed with the Keats set. Williams acted as matron to protect the patient from the well-meant excesses of his friends. He limited the visiting times, limited the visitors, reduced the poet's temperature, shielded him from the excessive bleeding his doctors swore would benefit him and, although no one had noticed, had not left the premises for his lodgings since he had fetched Keats from Hampstead. He was dog weary, occasionally snatching a nap in the back room when the grumbling Benyon was out of it. He woke to hear Taylor calling him.

'He needs laudanum,' he whispered. 'Do it without a fuss. Let it not be known. It is the only way he has been able to write since the sickness came so badly upon him.' Williams went out into the street, amazed that daily life went on. For days he had known nothing but Keats. He returned and gave the phial wordlessly.

'You feel it badly, don't you, Will?' Taylor's face was tired and drawn. 'But you serve him well. We do for him what we cannot do for Shakespeare and Chatterton because it is too late. Let us at least let Keats know the strength of our love and our belief in his genius.' Whether it was tiredness, or weakness because he had forgotten to eat, Williams was unable to stop the tears spilling down his face.

Benyon suddenly shouted that the carriage was at the door. He grabbed Keats' bag off Williams and limped importantly towards the vehicle.

'You'll come, Will,' said Taylor. 'We may need help. Put him in the carriage as comfortably as you can, it matters not how we sit.' Williams climbed inside to inspect the interior; it was reasonable but not luxurious. There was a chamber pot and a footwarmer, and the upholstery, although lumpy, had one good seat against the window facing the horses' heads. He heaved Keats in and settled him comfortably in that corner, putting the bag next to him to pinion him a little against the worst jolting on the poor roads which he knew led to the dock. Then he stood back and waited for the others to get in. Taylor settled opposite, leaving Williams to sit beside the poet. He sat down carefully, hardly daring to breathe. Looking sideways, he murmured, 'Are you comfortable John?'

The effort of boarding had exhausted Keats and he merely nodded. As the carriage rolled out of the city and across the bridge to the south, the water barely rippled and a faint sun broke through the dawn clouds.

'Junkets,' he whispered, wiping the pink phlegm from his mouth. 'I used to sign myself Junkets.' The brigantine rose and fell on the tide, a stiff breeze worrying the water and making the sails slap noisily as the sailors struggled to reef them; clouds were piling up like puffs of grey smoke. 'Byron would have liked that – watery milky whey – he called my poetry piss-a-bed.' Williams froze. He opened his mouth to provide an antidote when he realised that Keats was laughing.

'What chaos, Will – I'm dying, Fanny's alone – or is she? Even the weather's out of sorts.' In response the sky grew darker and a rumble of thunder growled in the distance. He began to cough and Williams passed him a linen towel. Handkerchiefs were little use these days. He put his arm round him and tried to wrap the blankets more firmly, but it was hard to find an anchor on the slight frame. The wrapping just fell away. At the other side of the deck Taylor leaned against the rigging. He could hear most of their conversation as the stiffened breeze wafted it.

'Failing to obtain the passport unnerves me,' said Taylor to Joseph Severn. 'I was never entirely convinced that you should be the one to accompany John, but you love him and you're available, the latter of which is not the case for Reynolds and Brown. Let's hope nothing else is forgotten.' He lowered his voice. 'But he seems cheerful, and Will is the best companion at the moment. He always knows what to say. Is it his youth?'

'It's love,' replied Severn. 'He's in love with Keats. We all are, a bit. I've never known a man draw friends like Keats. Will's youth and that instinct he has make him indispensable.' There was a splashing of oars and the passport bearer clambered over the side of the ship.

'Thank God,' cried Taylor. 'You've got it?'

'I have.' He waved a piece of official looking paper. He sat on a coil of ropes, getting his breath.

They eat their dinner with the captain on the deck as the ship sailed briskly towards Gravesend. There was fish and grilled mutton, chops and quantities of the claret Keats loved; Taylor had brought a case to last him the journey. In the vermilion shadows of the setting sun Keats appeared almost healthy; he had not been wracked by coughing during the meal and he made an immense effort to cheer his friends. He passed between his hands a white cornelian stone, sometimes pressing it to his face, smiling. He said quietly to Williams, 'It's Fanny's. A stone she cools her hands with when she's sewing. I can almost smell her on it.' He breathed as well as his lungs would let him, and then hid it in his sleeve.

They were pulling alongside at Gravesend. Williams knew that this was the moment of parting, where he would have to return to London on the stagecoach. Keats muttered, 'I'll go below. Help me, Will. I'll have Joseph until my life ends but you I will not see again.' Williams felt shock like a cold lump inside him. Settling Keats on the narrow bunk, he did not know how to take his leave. Suddenly he felt Keats' hand on his, pressing gently, kindly, as if he knew the turmoil in the younger man's heart.

'Thank you, Will,' he said tenderly. 'Don't grieve for me. I know what must be.' He closed his eyes and sank back onto the thin, grey pillow. Williams waited.

The breathing became easier as he slept. Slowly he withdrew his hand, and climbed the ladder back to the deck. He watched the fields of Kent pass in a blur as the stage coach slowly jogged back to London. He felt his life had ended.

CHAPTER 8

Monsieur Heger

'And was the pure passion you were describing,' said Charlotte slowly as they perambulated the garden for the twentieth time, 'was it Keats for Fanny or was it you for Keats?' She looked hard into Williams' face, her novelist's curiosity making her blunt. During the telling of the story he had been disturbed, his speech less coherent and the hand that was not holding hers within his arm gesturing agitatedly. 'Come, Will,' she said softly, 'I think you were half in love with Keats yourself!'

'As he was with easeful death,' replied Williams sadly. Then he smiled. 'You are most probably right. I never wrote another line of poetry except in the *Memorial* to him. Somehow I couldn't resist it, despite my good intentions not to.'

'Is it so bad?'

He sighed. 'Competent, but not inspired. I

struggled to be even competent. Pure poetry just flowed from him.' He manoeuvred her to a seat and then stood in front of her, and recited softly:

'Still do I see thee on the river's strand

Take thy last step upon thy native land-

Still feel the last kind pressure of thy hand.

I laid in wait to catch a glimpse of thee,

And plann'd that where'er thou wert that I might be.

I look'd on thee as a superior being

Whom I felt sweet content in merely seeing—'

Charlotte spread her hands in protest. 'Stop!' she cried. 'I can't bear any more. You were in love with him. I know all those symptoms, how keenly I remember doing all those things. Monsieur Heger – you know about Monsieur?'

Williams inclined his head but said nothing. He had heard gossip, on the publication of *Villette*. His virtue was listening rather than talking. He remained silent.

'He owned the pensionnat in Brussels which Emily and I went to.' She took a deep breath, leaning into herself with arms crossed, almost convulsed by the strength of her confession. 'I fell madly in love with him. He was married, very married, like you, lots of children and Madame a jealous serpent. He was very correct in our relationship, but at the time I could not see that my love, my behaviour, was improper.'

Sitting beside her, he asked, 'What drew you to him at first?'

'It may sound strange, but I think now that even with Emily with me I was very sick for home. I loved, still love, the house we lived in and my family. Papa has been very close to all of us; apart from a very short time at a ghastly school for clergy daughters—'

'I remember you used that in *Jane Eyre*. Incredibly compelling.'

'—he educated us at home,' she continued, as if he had not interrupted. He had noticed that when recounting her past life she often became so absorbed that she was unaware, seemingly alone. *She's almost writing this,* he thought. 'After Mama died he looked after six children—'

'Six?' Curiosity forced the interruption.

'Six,' she repeated slowly. 'That's the point. We had two more sisters, Maria and Elizabeth, and some well-meaning fellow clergyman persuaded him that with an income of £180 a year – he was a poor Irishman who had made his own way, so he had no private income like most Anglican parsons – it would be good to send the older daughters to a school which would guarantee them employment as governesses eventually.' She groaned. 'But they died from the atrocious conditions at the school. Maria died there, at Cowan Bridge, and he fetched Elizabeth back, but she died at home. He was completely heartbroken, sitting up with her night after night, and he never trusted anyone with us for many years.'

Williams sat in stunned silence. When he had read *Jane Eyre* at a sitting in its manuscript form he been swept away with the power and immediacy of the story, thinking it the work of Currer Bell's gifted imagination. He had had no idea that the intensity of emotion came from real life, worked into a dramatic story. Now he realised that its success came from truth.

'So Papa ran the parish and educated all of us himself,' she continued. 'He was a marvellous teacher, that is how he achieved his own education, teaching in hedge schools and tutoring in Ireland, being nurtured by a man who realised his potential. He was the eldest of ten children, and was twenty-five when he reached Cambridge.'

Will was impressed. 'He went to Cambridge? That's an extraordinary achievement for a poor young man.' He regretted his own lack of a university education; lack of money had never allowed it.

'He survived entirely on scholarships. Sometimes I think he barely ate except for the one meal allowed under the terms of his scholarships. He still barely eats! He was at Cambridge with Lord Byron and Wordsworth, and he got a better degree than any of them. We have a book at home which he bought with his prize money. It's inscribed "P Brontë his prize book for having always kept in the First Class St John's College Cambridge". So he extended his belief in education and his really brilliant mind to all of us, regardless of gender.' Her voice quavered. 'Can you understand how dear he is to me?'

'Indeed I can,' said Williams quietly, hardly daring to interrupt this story.

'So when Monsieur was teaching us French, and we were writing essays for him, I suppose I made a connection somehow with Papa. He had six children, Papa had six children—'

'And I have eight,' laughed Williams competitively.

'—and he was clever and appreciative of what little

talent I had. Just like Papa. Emily never had any of these feelings. She could live entirely in her mind, she didn't need people, except us, and not always us.' She paused. '*Wuthering Heights* isn't a novel about real people, is it Will? She created characters from scratch. I made them from people I knew.'

'And yourself?'

'And myself. I loved Monsieur for whatever reason, but now I really think it was because he was older, clever, and interested in my work, like Papa. It's very subjective.' She laughed and stopped, astonished. 'And it's nearly a description of you.'

'Indeed it is,' said Williams thoughtfully. 'Except that I don't want to be as correct as Monsieur. Let me tell you about your most intelligent critic, George Henry Lewes, my neighbour and longstanding friend. He has many children, has fallen deeply in love, and is interested in the work of a lady he loves passionately. But he's not going to behave correctly.'

'Mr Lewes!' exclaimed Charlotte in astonishment. 'But when I met him he talked to me proudly about his children! And when I visited you, you explained that they lived next door and all your children were friends.' She sniffed a little disdainfully. 'Where's the passion in that?' she said with not a little scorn.

'No idea,' said Williams. 'Sit quietly like a good girl and stop speculating and let me tell you about him. They've recently departed these shores, to more tolerant Weimar.'

CHAPTER 9

Good Neighbours

The autumn evening sun cast a pink light over the maturing bricks of the Kensington house; Williams sat beneath an ancient beech which had avoided the developers and made a softening feature in the garden of his house, part of a terrace enthusiastically rented by writers and others in need of a family home sufficiently removed from expensive London squares and crescents. Harvested from farm land, the garden still bore the marks of agriculture; vegetables grew well in the rich soil which had been so carefully tended for generations before the great speculative boom, and birds displaced from hedges crowded together in the remaining trees and woke the new inhabitants with a mighty dawn chorus during the spring and summer months. Not that Williams needed wakening; with eight children of various ages there was always someone who needed to get up early for work or to practise singing or piano; he had worked for so many years in a job he hated to keep them all in school and music lessons, and now, rescued by publisher George Smith to become the trusted reader at Smith Elder, he revelled in his easy contact with writers and the friends who had kept him sane by passing theatre and book reviewing jobs to him. Now one of his oldest friends lived next door, in fact had tipped him off that the house next to his was becoming vacant.

Suddenly focused by the smell of a bonfire, he left his tree stump and tactfully shuffled his feet in the dry fallen leaves to announce his presence. A short man stood by the fire, wiry, dark curly hair receding and, now that he turned to Williams, brilliant, dark, intelligent eyes seeking his.

'I'm keeping out of the way,' he mouthed softly, stirring the embers with an iron pole and nodding his head in the direction of the house. Schubert hung in the air from the piano within, melancholy pervading the open air. 'He's here again.'

Williams winced. George's problem with Thornton Hunt distressed him probably as much it did Lewes. Raising his shaggy brows and his shoulders, he said, 'I'm not sure what you can do. He's been our friend for so long. After all, my Thornton is named after him. Yours too. I never thought...'

'How would we?' replied Lewes. George Lewes, sharp critic, editor, researching scientist, respected reviewer, attractive to women despite his ugliness, was at a loss to deal with his own domestic problems.

'I suppose it was those days in Bayswater which sowed the seeds,' Lewes continued. He left his fire to smoulder fragrantly and rested on a wooden bench riddled with woodworm and green with moss. Williams, lightly swinging his long legs over the stunted hedge which was the boundary between their two houses, joined him. They sat watching the disappearing sun, two old friends content to remain silent until the right words came. The Schubert continued, rather brilliantly played; from out of Williams' house came a tall, fair girl, her dark blue gown and light shawl throwing her handsome face into relief.

'That's so beautiful,' she said, coming to stand by the fence. 'Good evening Mr Lewes. I wish I played like Mrs Lewes.'

'You do,' said Williams kindly, Lewes nodding agreement. 'Fanny, you know you do.'

Pleasure at praise showed in Fanny's face. 'I don't mean to interrupt,' she said, 'but you should come in, Papa, it's getting cold.'

'A few minutes,' replied Williams. 'George and I have fat to chew.' A crash, followed by a howl of pain, issued from the upper storeys of the Williams house. 'Go and tell those boys to calm down,' he said, 'please.' The girl laughed and went inside. He was proud of his family. They had all survived the ravages of childhood infections, were good looking and intelligent, good humoured, and even kind to their father and mother. What more could one ask for?

'Bayswater.' Williams wrenched himself back into the present. He smiled, although Lewes did not. 'People used to call it the Phalanstery. Our experiment in communal living. Most believed we were sharing our wives, rather than trying to release them from domestic oppression by sharing tasks and children.'

Lewes rose and thwacked the fire which flared, spitting, cracking on its unknown contents. He sighed, leaning on the pole.

'Thornton was there, you, me, our wives and children,' he said. 'It was good, though difficult in such a small house. I suppose in our small experiment we were confused by the example of our great liberal aristocrats. It's easier when you have money and servants like Byron, and genius, of course, to bring in the money. Shelley too – when I think how young he was when he left his poor Harriet with their child, and went jolting over the mountain roads to France with Mary Godwin pregnant and only seventeen. It makes Thornton appear positively mature!'

Williams rose and shivered slightly. He was not sure if it was the now colder night air or the thoughts of those dangerous times past when he wrestled – successfully – with the temptations of communal living in Bayswater. Certainly Thornton Hunt had not; he was not sure about Lewes. Williams and his wife Margaret had been glad to reduce expenses by sharing the house after the collapse of his business; but he and Margaret had been aware of the undercurrents and had soon preferred penury to adultery, and quietly moved out.

'Come,' he said, laying a hand on Lewes's shoulder, already rounded from stooping over his varied writing pursuits, 'come inside and have a pipe.' He could see it would be a welcome invitation to delay entering his own house and the music making of Thornton Hunt and Agnes Lewes.

'Thank you. You're a tactful, sensitive man, Will, always have been.' They climbed the stone steps up to the garden door, Lewes pausing behind him, halfway up. He looked up at Will, his irregular features, ravaged by small pox and past carbuncles, expressing fleeting pain. 'Four children, Will, she's had with Thornton. What do people think of me? Thing is, I'm still fond of her – not in love of course – but we have children together, and we've had good times...'

'We've all had good times,' said Will firmly, guiding him up into the parlour which overlooked the garden, at this time a comparatively calm room in this busy house, 'it's keeping it going when the times are not so good that takes the skill.'

Fanny came in and asked if there was anything they needed. Will reached for her hand.

'No, my dear. I'm sure you've had a hard day with your pupils assaulting your ears with their singing and piano. Go and sit with your mother and let's hope the younger ones are in bed.' He could hardly discuss the Lewes' marriage in front of her, although he loved her cheerful company. Inside they settled on either side of a small fire which Williams kicked into life from dying embers and started to load and light their pipes. The room was shabby but charming. Books lined the walls and teetered in piles on the floor and late roses spilled out of a humble jar on the piano. There was a desk piled with papers against the wall opposite the fire where no doubt Williams wrote his reviews and some sad letters to aspiring authors. He relished the letters to the blazing talents but he had been told by one aspiring lady that no one could think more cruelly than he, no one wound more deeply when it came to the pen and ink contradiction of his mild words. He sighed. Business and talent; hard compromises. He sighed. He suddenly realised that Lewes had his large dark head in his hands.

'George?'

George creaked in the old chair and sat upright again. His small frame, encased in a dark suit with colourful cravat, seemed to tremble for a moment. Then he stood up with his back to the fire, one hand in his pocket, the other still grasping a now dead pipe, eyes fixed on the worn carpet. 'I've got to do something. I should never have given the last child my name on the birth certificate. I've been told it condones the adultery and I will never therefore be able to divorce Agnes. She and Thornton have something serious between them – God knows what after all these years – but I can't go on living with her with Thornton coming and going. He had another child by his wife within three months of Agnes's last by him! He doesn't see it as a difficulty.'

'Why would he?' Will breathed deeply into his pipe bowl, filling the air with a deep sensual pungency, the tobacco a gift from Thackeray to soothe Williams after *Vanity Fair* had gone to another publisher. 'Why on earth would he? Leigh Hunt embraced the theories of Rousseau and believed that there should be no restraints or boundaries in his children's lives. Thornton went with his parents to Italy to live with the Shelleys and Byron when he was just a child. He saw how they lived. Scribbled on Byron's walls and answered him back; Mrs Hunt told the great Lord that there was nothing more absurd than a peer of the realm, and a poet, making such a fuss about three or four children disfiguring the walls in a few rooms. He called them Yahoos, Hottentots, Blackguards. Thornton heard Byron taunting his mother, saying his morals had been criticised, whereupon his mother replied it was the first time she had ever heard of them! That's hardly a background which is going to produce a respectful, conventional, restrained child!'

'And he spent his early years in prison with his father when Leigh was incarcerated for criticising our late fat monarch. Despite the flowers and the piano and visitors, including Byron, it was a wretched place for a child to be. He's been raised with rebellion in his mother's milk.'

Do you remember the poem Charles Lamb wrote for Thornton?' recalled Lewes. 'He called him his "Favourite Child". It was something like:

"Gates that close with iron roar

Have been to thee thy nursery door;

Walls contrived for giant sin

Have hemmed thy faultless weakness in."

Poor little scrap. Yes, I can see your point. After all that he's not going to obey the rules if they don't suit him.'

'Why now?' asked Will, looking at him intently. 'You've put up with it so long and,' he lowered his voice, glancing at the slightly open door, 'made your own arrangements, and Agnes has been affable, kind, and happy with her babies, whoever's they were.' Despite himself he laughed at this. 'I suppose you never absolutely knew? So why now?'

George got up and stood in the circle of light cast

by the single candle Fanny had placed on a low table before she left them. One of the younger boys of the household crashed down the stairs towards the front door and the candle flared up in the draught, momentarily exposing the deep lines etched into his face. 'Things change,' he said quietly. 'I can't tell you how yet. I'm not sure myself, but I know I have to leave and be out of a dead marriage soon.' It was as if a sudden resolve overtook him. 'Thanks Will. I'll go now. May I leave by your front door rather than the garden? Then I can enter my house noisily.' He mimed a little noisy swagger. Williams smiled and took a cigar out of a box on the mantel shelf. 'Here, take this,' he said. 'They're good for ruminating, and they'll smell it as you enter. Take a light.' He took a splint from the glass dish above the fireplace and lit it in the fire. Cigar in mouth, flare in hand, George Lewes left by the front door, his head transformed by the redness of the setting sun into a fiery globe.

Outside on the rough track in front of the terraced houses it was cooler. He stood against the wall surrounding the mansion opposite; small animals scuttled in the dried leaves and birds, late to bed, chuntered above him, an odd owl hoot starting in the distance. George surveyed the outside of his house, faint candlelight glowing in some of the unshuttered windows; a busy house with babies and children, and nursemaids, giving Agnes time to be confined for births and play the piano. He flicked cigar ash as it died and then watched the tobacco burn and glow in the dark. Filling his lungs over and over again, he at last re-crossed the track, and noisily turning the handle, he entered the hall, creating an arabesque with his cigar in the hall to spread its fine aroma and announce his coming. He clattered his stick down on a table to give them more warning. The Schubert had just resolved into its dominant, final chord. Lewes entered his drawing room and stood at the open door, looking from his wife to her lover. 'She's good, isn't she?' he said, ignoring Agnes, addressing Thornton, who lounged in a low chair near the piano.

'Very good,' smiled Thornton, his simian features relaxing into a pleasant grin. 'But we always knew that, didn't we?' He laughed and rose, kissing Agnes lightly on the top of her fair head. 'But I must be off. *The Leader* is due out and near enough finished but I need to check the proofs. See you there in the morning, George?' George nodded. As co-founder with Thornton of *The Leader* he had filed his literary copy earlier that week. He stood back to let him pass into the hall. A maid, following the telepathy of her class, had appeared with his hat and stick. An ironic low bow to her raised a blush, and, satisfied that his technique still worked with women, he went towards the door. 'Till the morning then.' And he disappeared into the fast-falling night.

Agnes began another *Impromptu* but George crossed the room and began to lower the piano lid. Raising her pretty eyebrows and sitting back when she realised his intention, she stopped playing and turned towards him. 'Something wrong?'

'Indeed,' he said, 'something is wrong. Really wrong and this time it has to change. I'm going to move into rooms not far away.'

'Really?' she said. She was still pretty, despite the many pregnancies, although plump. She was not a fool and quite able to sense the urgency of his mood.

'Because of Thornton? Why? Do you want a divorce?'

'Can't do that. I'm on the children's birth certificates and that condones the adultery. I'm not going to talk about it,' he said. 'We know each other so well that you must have anticipated a break at some point. Why it's now is my decision. I'll support you well, and all the children, although it would be good if Thornton could help a little with his...'

'Of course he will,' she said defensively. 'He always has... a bit.'

'It may have to be more than a bit, but I'll sort it out with him. Our boys will soon be old enough to go abroad to school, that's what I'd like, a real broad education, with science and languages. The other four will remain with you here, or with Thornton's family if that's what he wishes.' He stopped, moving towards the window, blank with darkness now. 'I love them all,' he said gruffly. 'I think the youngest think I am their father, maybe all of them, I don't know what you tell them. I live here and Thornton doesn't, so how can they work it out? But not any more.'

Agnes rotated on the piano stool so that she was facing him, stretching out her legs under the blue dress, which was still flattering, its prettiness undiminished by the many easings it had received to accommodate her changing figure. It rustled faintly as she turned.

'Do you have to? We all get along so well and you have your life away from here. Can't you just leave be?' She smiled up at him, mature, confident, relaxed. They had been together for over ten years and they liked each other, although love and desire had died years ago. They were lucky to have made it this far.

But Thornton stirred in her something she could not deny. If there had to be a choice…

'No,' said George. He was finding it harder than he expected, as if she were going to die and he would have to cope with a bereavement. 'No, no, no.' He spread his fine, ink stained hands out in front of him to steady his resolve, blotting her out. Looking around the room at the familiar objects, cheerfully moved from one house to another, china, pictures, books, children's leavings, he had to brace himself. All this would be gone, together with his easy access to his greatest loves, the children. 'No. It's time. Things change. I need to go.' Before he was influenced by the loveliness of her intelligent blue eyes and her attractive familiarity, he turned and abruptly left the room. The outer door slammed, rendering the maid redundant.

Agnes shrugged and rotated. For a while she sat still. She felt, unusually, disturbed, dispirited. The balance she had to maintain with men, music, and children sometimes threatened to overwhelm her, but generally she managed to be pleasant, witty and loving to all. She smiled as she thought of the sketch William Thackeray had done of her playing the piano with George and Thornton watching her. A perceptive man; but he had left out the children, possibly the hardest juggle of all. She started the *Impromptu* again, music obliterating cares.

CHAPTER 10

Wider Horizons

Charlotte had suggested that the next day they should meet in the Chapter Coffee House, near St Paul's Cathedral, familiar to her from staying there with her father and sister on the way to Brussels, and even more to Mr Brontë from his undergraduate days. Originally the haunt of writers, critics, and wits, who found its proximity to Paternoster Row convenient for the concentration of publishers and booksellers there, it had changed over the years to a sedate but shabby refuge where strangers from the country and small market towns welcomed its protection from the roar outside of people, animals, and the bells tolling sonorously at St Paul's. Smoke and soot remained outside, replaced within by comforting pipes and cigars.

Williams found Charlotte on a window seat, peering shortsightedly at the gloom outside. She rose when he came in and came eagerly towards him, putting out her hands to take his: he held them tightly before they moved to two vacant chairs by the fire. She wore a heavy woollen cloak, obviously the work of a Haworth tailor who worked closely with his weaving neighbours. He noticed the drawn threads about the hem where she had tangled with undergrowth, as she raced to the train across the fields from Haworth. She pushed it off her shoulders as the heat of the fire spread. Tired clerics snoozed around them; the bustle of London soon overtook their provincial souls and bodies, and Charlotte remembered her father snoring a little in this room when the two sisters stayed here with him on their way to Brussels, until poked sharply awake by Emily. The kindly waiter had remembered her, drawing her attention to the visitors' book which contained all their signatures, including Papa's from before he went to Cambridge. Appreciative, but barely concentrating, she stretched in the florid overstuffed armchair and, taking off her bonnet, dropped it carelessly on the floor. Her colour, despite the coldness of the day, was high. Williams could barely hear what she was saying.

'Poor Mr Lewes! I had no idea. He is my best, most stimulating critic. The only serious, accurate writer on *Jane Eyre*. He said to me that we had much in common as we had both written "naughty" books. His really was naughty, in the French sense,' she laughed and sat back, firelight warming her features, her voice strengthening, 'mine naughty because it was thought daughters, wives, and servants should not read it. I was cross at the time.' She glanced at Williams. 'But then I often am,' he nodded agreeably, 'and when I met him I nearly wept because he so closely resembled Emily. The prominent mouth, dark challenging eyes, features, even the expression, were all hers.' She struggled with tears. 'And all the time he was living like Mr Rochester—'

'Hang on a bit,' said Williams mildly, 'Agnes is hardly the mad woman in the attic. I've known them for years and can assure you there's nothing Gothic in it. She is a merry lady with great musical talent but a penchant for literary men, regardless of marital status.' The waiter came to remove the coffee pot, but lingered a while over this interesting statement. He fed the fire with sea coal. The coals shifted and glowed; peace settled in the room, now empty except for them.

'So what did he want to do?' she asked softly. 'When he left Agnes, what did he want to do?'

'I'll tell you,' said Williams. He had decided the harsh day merited a muffin; Charlotte had daintily refused, but seemed to regret it when the fragrant buttery creation arrived. 'Would you like a bit?' he asked, suspending a yeasty smelling piece on a fork. He was rewarded with the sight of her daintiness vanishing in a hungry gobble. In the absence of the waiter he threw another log on the fire. 'I'll tell you. He has a grand passion for a lady who is not his wife. She's called Marian Evans, she came from Coventry to London after the death of her father, and got reviewing work, and published some articles.'

Charlotte's forehead wrinkled. 'Is that all she does?'

'No,' said Williams, carefully watching her reactions. 'She's at present editing the *Westminster Review* and doing it very well indeed. She has prodigious talent as a writer, and I—'

'And you should know,' Charlotte finished the sentence for him. 'Yes, indeed you can spot a writer.

How would I ever I have managed without you recommending *Jane Eyre* to Mr Smith?'

'When I've spoken to her, as I have on many occasions, she has confided to me that she longs to write fiction.'

'A serious competitor?' Charlotte tried to sound casual.

'Could indeed be, once she gets going.' Williams observed the faint shadow of jealousy that hovered on Charlotte's face, and reflected on the vulnerability of writers. 'But different, so there's room for both of you. But I've told her she'll have to change her name, probably to a male one, but mainly to distance herself from the reviewing. By the way, why did you and your sisters choose Bell when you first tried to publish?'

'Actually, that's very interesting now you mention it,' replied Charlotte, her eyes fixed on the glowing fire as if she was seeing other places and things in it. 'We kept our own initials but Bell was Mr Nicholls's name. He's called Arthur Bell Nicholls. We liked him in the end: he was so good to Papa when he had cataracts, and he would walk the dogs for miles on the moors when we had colds or the weather was abominable as it so often is up there. Isn't that strange, given that we're talking about him really, all the time?'

'Strange indeed,' smiled Williams. '"There's more things in heaven and earth..."'

'What might she choose?' Charlotte ignored this scholarly aside and rushed on. She needed to keep this name in her head so that she could check the rival's progress later without seeming to ask too many questions. 'She could take her lover's name, George –

not that Mr Nicholls was my lover, of course,' she added hastily, 'and we kept the B for Brontë, so she might keep the E for Evans...'*

'You're speculating again. Just be a good girl and sit quietly and I will tell you all about it.'

*She did. She published her fiction under the name George Eliot.

CHAPTER 11

Ménage à Quatre

Williams pulled up the collar of his black great coat while hanging onto his hat with his other hand. The wind funnelled up the Strand and showered walkers with that peculiar London dust composed of well ground horse droppings and the fine grit of badly laid roads. His eyes stung and he tried to hide his head within his collar without dangerously losing his vision. One careless step and he would be under someone's wheels. It was starting to rain and he knew that by the time he had completed his errand he would be walking back through a slurry of mud with a stronger stench than the dry dust he now battled with. Reaching number 142 he pulled heavily three times on the bell, then stood back, hunched against the cold as he listened to its far away jangle in the bowels of the house.

He knew the response would not be swift: Susanna Chapman's housekeeping skills were known throughout literary London for their eccentricities, and it was only her husband's connections with the publishing world which kept their boarding house well stocked with literary ladies and visiting Americans. The shop door was separate from the house and brown parcels of books were at that minute being unloaded from a flat cart. The skinny horse, ears well back, hung its head and waited. Williams waited. At last the door opened and a small, bedraggled girl, wrapped in an apron made for a bigger maid, looked enquiringly at him.

'Mistress is not at home,' she lisped. She had said it many times to protect her careworn employer.

'It is not your mistress, but your master I have come to see.' Williams smiled at the child. He worried about the children employed as house maids and kitchen maids all over London who were scarcely old enough to leave their families, if they had them; loosed upon a dangerous world for the sake of three meals a day, they endured their hardships as a dog endures if he is unlucky enough to have an unkind master. He had never forgotten waking in the night to the sobbing of their own thirteen-year-old maid, alone in an attic room, the desolation floating down the stairs, misery filtering into his own bedroom. He had lain listening and was about to get up to do something about it when his wife placed a restraining hand on his shoulder.

'Don't. They have to get used to it. They are all homesick. Leave be.'

And he had lain on his back until the sobbing ceased when the sun eventually slit the heavy curtains. Children. His own, others, it was a constant, nagging preoccupation.

'The master is in,' replied the child, 'but I'll have to see if he'll see you. He has his work. Who shall I say it is?' She pushed the door until it was almost closed and he heard her feet pattering upstairs, then a pause and back down again. 'He says you may come up,' she said, this time smiling at him, her blue eyes friendly. Closing the door behind him, she led him into the house. The hallway, with its wide wooden stairs, was dark and smelt of cabbage and boiled meat; the light was better on the landing where the weak sun shone through a tall arched window. The shop noise was very faintly audible through the walls, muffled voices, a chair scraping, thumps of packets being moved about. For a moment he was a seventeen-year-old again. The girl led him into the drawing room.

'Here's the gentleman, sir,' and she pattered away down the stairs to the basement.

The man at the desk in the window was tall, young, and beautiful. His curly dark hair fell over his eyes. His smile lit up a finely boned face. Williams liked the appearance but was wary of the man. John Chapman, known to his friends as Byron for his looks and his lifestyle, jumped up from his writing table and extended his hand. Before Williams could take it a stout, harassed woman blundered into the room, her untidy greying hair escaping from a limp white cap. Hot behind her came a younger, prettier woman with an unpleasant expression. They both stopped dead with surprise. The older woman burst into tears. Williams retreated behind the piano in embarrassment. Chapman took the older woman, his wife, by the arm.

'My dear Susanna,' he said soothingly, stroking her

shoulder, 'be still. What is the matter?' Over her head he raised one finger and his eyebrows warningly at the younger woman, then looked away, away from the fury in her face. Susanna buried her face in her apron and wept.

'You know, you know!' she sobbed convulsively. 'Why must I endure her everywhere in my house? Why do you want her with you all the time—'

He took her expertly in his arms, smoothing her untidy hair. Across the room Elisabeth bridled. 'She's the children's governess,' he whispered, 'she has to be about the house. But I'll make everything better.' The sobs ceased. Susanna looked up into her husband's beautiful brown eyes. She melted. 'And tonight we will be together.' The whisper was not so soft that Williams could not hear. 'And now some coffee for Mr Williams,' he said cheerfully, problem solved for him. 'Send Elisabeth with it, don't do the stairs yourself. You are the mistress of the house.' He glanced significantly across the room, willing Elisabeth to silence. In return he received another furious glance.

She lingered after the wife had departed, but Chapman ignored her. Finally she left, closing the door as noisily as she could without actually slamming it. Williams placed his hat on the piano, came out into the war zone and took a deep breath.

'If the moment is inconvenient…'

'Will, it's a real pleasure to see you!'

'I had hoped to talk about the Booksellers' Association, and the meeting you're planning. George Smith is anxious to know your intentions.'

Chapman ceased to look like a devious animal and

became a business man. 'I'm determined to go ahead with it.' He was serious, involved. *How like the duality of Leigh Hunt,* thought Williams; Hunt's reputation as a brilliant journalist and generous helper of young literary talent was besmirched by the embarrassment of his constant need to borrow money. Chapman's talent as a publisher was equally clouded by his womanising.

'The meeting is soon. Dickens will chair the meeting. We'll hold it here like one of our evening parties. I'm absolutely determined. I did nothing wrong – the agreement did not cover imports to America. I was within my rights to sell them at cost with a little commission. For that my bookseller's ticket was withdrawn. I shall fight it.' There was an altercation on the stairs, a dropped tray clanging through the house like a gate in hell. Chapman returned to his sheepish look.

'Perhaps we should forget the coffee.' Williams waved a hand. 'Inevitably,' he continued cheerfully, 'there are clashes when running business, a boarding house, and a home...' He paused, suddenly smiling boyishly at Williams. 'You know I am not the best of husbands... I try, but I do so love women.' There was a perceptible spring in his step as he turned his back, and, hands in pockets, looked out of the window onto the bustling Strand. The rain had started in earnest and people and horses shone dully. He turned back, grinning, and shrugged. 'You know how it is.'

Williams didn't really. He had been married for well over twenty years to his wife Margaret, and apart from a single aberration in a whorehouse after a night with a novelist he did not take on, he had remained undeviatingly faithful. His eight children, born in a period of twenty years, were testament to a reasonably active sex life; after the birth of Anna, Margaret had always been too ill for further pleasure. He loved his children, thanked whatever Providence there was that every one of his had survived and took enormous pleasure in their artistic interests; the thought of losing their respect and company had kept him celibate. Living next door to the Leweses had shown him the complications of the open marriage.

Chapman looked closely at him as he emerged from this reverie. 'You don't approve, do you Will?' He was like a little boy trying to persuade a parent that his errant behaviour was all right really. Indicating a chair for Williams, he sat backwards on an upright chair himself and rested his chin on his arms along the spandrel. 'I try not to hurt anyone,' he said charmingly, 'I love them all.'

'And they all love you,' replied Williams dryly. 'The town is full of men like you, thinking that they are making their wives and mistresses happy by loving them all. My experience with women,' and he shot Chapman a humorous glance, 'is that they love totally and seldom want to share.'

'Your experience?' asked Chapman, surprised.

'In the books they write. I read their novels. Some of them we publish. But all of them, from *Jane Eyre* to the one I've most recently turned down, tell me that they love singly and want to be loved like that themselves. How can you think otherwise?'

'I want to think otherwise.' He sighed. 'There are not many men like you, Will, decent and selfless. The rest of us find it harder.' He rose and went back to the window. 'Look out there – hundreds of women, endless possibilities; you cannot deny that they respond, respond with great enthusiasm,' he muttered with not a little relish.

'Often out of inexperience and hope for love.' Williams joined him at the window. 'And that one,' he nodded towards the street, where a tall young woman was battling with an umbrella and her wet billowing skirts as she made her way towards the Chapman's door, 'that one – is she still responding?'

'How have you heard that?' Chapman was astonished. They continued to watch the woman, her face now exposed by the closed umbrella, heavy but intelligent with a softness in her expression which illuminated the plainness. She was tall, sinuous, carefully dressed. She disappeared into the street door. They heard it thud shut from where they stood. A low voice in the hall, footsteps on the stairs. Another door opened and shut. 'I didn't realise everyone knew.' Chapman almost blushed.

Williams continued seriously, 'You more than anyone know the web of literary London. Your own Friday nights encourage meetings with cubs as well as lions. And those who come who believe in free love often make it seem normal.'

Chapman's face grew pensive. 'Sadly, Susanna will not agree to an open ménage. I've often pointed out to her the happiness of the households where neither husband nor wife own each other, but are free to do as they please, to love whom they please. That would be very suitable for me.'

'Where I have observed it,' replied Williams, returning to the depths of the room and gazing into the fire which now burned brightly after the little girl had struggled upstairs with coal and wood and quietly serviced it, 'it is not an easy path for everyone. I lived next door to George and Agnes Lewes. I cannot say that the open marriage even at that point seemed to be without jealousy or recrimination. Beliefs in freedom are sometimes at odds with personal emotion. Shelley discovered that when his Harriet threw herself in the Serpentine.' For a split second Chapman's face clouded. It soon passed. 'Which is why I mention Miss Evans.'

Chapman said defensively, 'She's a young woman, of independent means, with her hair up and out on the town here by her own decision. I merely seek to help her…'

'No you don't,' said Williams firmly, 'you seek two things: her in your bed when neither Susanna nor Elisabeth is there, and her to work for you on the *Westminster Review*, which since she's been doing it has been excellent – far in advance of anything you produced.'

Chapman laughed. 'She's told me not to write for it myself. She thinks I should stick to the accountancy. It's a bit humiliating really, being told you're not good enough by the woman assistant editor when you own the magazine.'

'Exactly,' said Williams with the air of man who has had his point made for him. 'You use her intellect and talent and reward her with sex rather than paying her as you would a man.' He stopped, not regretting what he had said but feeling that Chapman needed time to take it in. There was a silence. Beethoven burst from another piano somewhere in the house.

Chapman said: 'I thought you liked me.'

'I do. But I don't like the way you treat this woman. I know her from your evenings. I've talked to her at length when she first came and knew no one. Young women talk to me – they see me as safe, like their fathers. She told me a lot about hers, her difficulties with him and leaving home. She was worried that his death would remove restrictions from her she dearly needed to have. She's needy, emotionally needy. She's also brilliant and analytical. You're abusing her vulnerability. When I see a talent like hers I like it even less when a man takes advantage.' He sat back in his chair and waited, his arms spread with a relaxation he did not really feel. Nothing happened. Yellow fog started to spread through the gas light in the Strand. Suddenly the Beethoven stopped; footsteps came rapidly towards the door. When it opened the tall young woman stood there, her slim body at odds with her heavy face; her dark hair was drawn back but untidy. She wasn't beautiful at all, but in her presence and her fine blue eyes there was enough passion to dissipate her heavy looks.

'John—' her voice was deep and attractive, musical, retaining vestiges of its Midlands vowels, but hesitant. *Probably only in his presence*, thought Williams. *She simply won't know what he's up to*. Chapman drew her into the room.

'My dear Marian, you know Mr Williams.'

'I do.' The blue eyes settled on him. 'How else would I have endured your Friday evenings if there had not been one person there who was not so obsessed with himself that he had time to talk to me? You were kind, Mr Williams, and I seem to remember known as a great talent when it comes to discovering literature. It is you who knows Miss Brontë so well, who plucked her out of obscurity. And you knew Keats too.' Williams smiled shyly and took her hand, removing her from Chapman's heavy grasp and settled her in a chair by the fire. She turned to look at Chapman. 'I came because I can wait no longer for your decision on the April edition. It has to go to press soon. It's no good my playing the piano while I wait for you to you talk and dine—'

'You play so beautifully,' said the errant owner of the *Westminster Review*. 'I have to listen, work takes second place.'

'Simpleton,' she replied quietly. 'The work has to be done and done properly. I can't bear anything in my name to be shoddy. It must be right.'

'But it's not in your name,' laughed Chapman. 'No one knows it's by you so just do what you can in the time.' There was silence. Marian took a deep breath and stood up. Tears in her eyes.

'Let me know your decision,' she said abruptly. She pulled her shawl tightly across her shoulders and went out.

'You are amazing,' breathed Will, surprised at a sudden rush of anger. 'How can you treat her like that? You abuse her integrity as a woman and as a writer. That's what she cares about.'

'No she doesn't,' laughed Chapman. 'All she wants is to be beautiful. They all do. The last time she cried was when I visited her at the Brays in

Coventry and I told her how important beauty was to me. Don't berate me. It's not my fault if women are vain.'

Williams sighed. He was remembering a conversation with George Smith about Charlotte. Smith had felt that Charlotte would have given all her talent to be beautiful. Williams felt it was deeper than that. The fight for recognition as writers in a man's world obsessed by female beauty made them yearn for beauty to get it out of the way.

'Well,' said Chapman, 'it's no use her thinking things will change. If you really want to know she won't come to my bed since I returned to London. When she started to press me warmly about my feelings for her and when I told her that I love both Susanna and Elisabeth in different ways she got all frosty and she hasn't been near me since. She does the work and plays the piano. She keeps close company with Herbert Spencer, and gives him admiration for his philosophical writings, but she's still recovering from his avowals of loving physical beauty. So they walk on the terrace opposite, gaze at the river and discuss Life and Philosophy and visit Richmond and Kew and still she finds no one to love her!'

'You *are* a bastard,' said Williams softly. 'At least you should wish her well for all the good she's doing the *Westminster Review*.' Abruptly, he picked up his hat and gloves from the piano. 'I'll tell George about the meeting. I have to wish you well though the system involves practices I find repugnant: as I do your treatment of Miss Evans. Good day to you.' He left the room without waiting for a response from Chapman, who was still standing looking slightly ashamed when Elisabeth, taking advantage of Mrs Chapman's absence at Fortnum's, sidled in with his coffee and a meaning look.

CHAPTER 12

Literary London

Williams had avoided Chapman after this exchange, and kept contact mainly through the Friday night parties that he hosted, which anyone of significance in literary London attended; sometimes a hundred people heaved in the drawing room and the little boudoir rooms overlooking the Strand. The chandeliers' dim glass needed a good clean, far beyond the housekeeping skills of Susanna Chapman and her little maid, but they cast a flattering light with their dusty glow. The room was warm beyond comfort from the fires in the contiguous rooms; faces shone sweatily and voices rose in a continuous soft roar of opinions, beliefs, and judgements. The food and drink were meagre, but the company scintillating.

Williams was standing in the big window with George Smith and George Lewes, Lewes the centre of a large group of black-coated men, many of whom wore brightly coloured cravats to signify their artistic inclinations. They were writers, reviewers, hacks trying to write for the many periodicals which flooded the huge market that had grown with improved literacy following compulsory education. George Lewes told his racy stories in swift colloquial French with huge laughter bellowing around him. Williams quite envied him: they were of similar backgrounds, non-university men who had made their own way, but Lewes's education, or at least sojourns, abroad had given him a breadth of European culture which Williams felt he himself lacked. He sighed. As he turned to deposit the ash from his trembling cigar in a strategically placed standing ash tray, he met the eyes of Marian Evans. She had been moving between groups, absorbed then distracted. She smiled and moved towards him. As she did so, she returned her gaze to its original focus, George Lewes. Her face relaxed and became unexpectedly beautiful in the dim light, her expression inscrutable.

'He's good for a laugh, isn't he, Mr Williams?' she said softly. Her voice was very attractive, intimate, the Midland's vowels oddly assertive. 'I wish I had his learning.'

'Exactly what I was thinking myself, Miss Evans,' he replied, guiding her across the room to a recently vacated chair. Her black dress showed her glossy brown hair to advantage. 'He spent a lot of time abroad and he speaks five languages fluently. Such a scientist too, a really enquiring, genuine intellectual.'

'I first met him in Jeff's bookshop in Piccadilly,' she said, settling her skirts out of range of the fire. 'Quite appropriate, don't you think? I know him better now. I realise he is a man of heart and conscience wearing a mask of flippancy.' As if to endorse the latter part of her statement a gust of laughter burst on the other side of the room. Williams looked hard at her.

'I've known him for years and been his neighbour. You couldn't be more right!'

'By the way,' she said, 'I've still got your copy of Keats's *Endymion*. It meant so much to read it after you told me the circumstances.' Williams flinched slightly, perched on the arm of a chair opposite.

'I think I dine out on that too much,' he said ruefully. 'You must forgive an old man.'

'No need for forgiveness. But you must have it back. It's in my room. Let's get it. These parties always spill through the whole house so you never know who you will find there.'

Pushing their way through the garrulous men and women now thronging the corridors in order to escape the heat of the main rooms, they eventually came to closed doors. Opening one, Marian drew him in. He left the door open behind him. He had been here often before, when sent by George Smith to negotiate reviews of their publications in the *Westminster Review*. Her room had a piano, topped with well-thumbed scores; she played very well and found it an aid to thinking about the writing and editing she was engaged on. She was rarely at her desk but preferred the sofa, where she often sat with her hair streaming down behind her and her long legs drawn up underneath her. It was here she had told him about her father and the Big Row when she refused to go to church in Coventry, which propelled her to London alone.

Her books lined the walls and had a tidy, organised appearance so that she soon found his copy of Keats.

'I wanted to give it back,' she murmured. 'I'd hate anything so lovely to go astray. I thought I'd tell you...' Here she leaned behind him and closed the door, the noise outside suddenly dying away. 'I thought I'd tell you that I'll be moving soon.' She struggled slightly, her usual fluency restrained.

Williams felt shocked but glad. 'Not too far away, I hope? And we'll still see you at these parties?'

She looked at him from beneath hair which had struggled out of its pins, eyes smiling but telling nothing. 'I might go to Labassecour,' she said.

He opened his mouth to speak but shut it again. Labassecour was Brussels, the fictional town where Charlotte Brontë had sent Lucy Snowe for her romantic assignation with Paul Emmanuel, a character based on Constantin Heger, a married man. She was telling him something.

Williams remained silent, wary.

Handing him the book she planted a kiss lightly on his cheek, her free hand patting his shoulder.

'You've been such a comfort to me,' she murmured. 'I always sensed an integrity in you which is often blissfully absent in our literary colleagues. I'll always remember you with great affection. You're always kind.' She stopped, remembering. 'No, not always,' and she threw her head back and pealed with laughter. 'Poor Eliza Linton. I remember coming into the room just as you had told her the best thing to do with her manuscript was to throw it on the fire! But it was true, I read it.' She smiled again, and, lightly guiding him, she opened the door and he was gently dismissed. He pushed his way back along the corridor, bumping against Dickens as he went, who sounded as if he were recruiting for his next theatrical production. Back in the noisy, smoky salon he glanced across to George Lewes again, still entertaining a large circle, laughter gusting around him. Lewes caught his eye and winked across at him, collusively, as if acknowledging a kinship above the rest of the room's occupants. He smiled back and made for the door, starting down the staircase, oblivious to the cooking smells and clangs from the kitchen. Reaching the street door, he put his hat on his head, then tilted it back with his stick, and let out a low whistle.

'George is on the move,' he said to himself with a chuckle, 'and now Miss Evans! What can that mean?' And he tossed his hat in the air, caught it and laughed out loud.

CHAPTER 13

Getting to Know the Hunts

There was dead silence in the parlour of the Chapter Coffee House. Charlotte looked stunned.

'But I... But she...'

Williams laughed at her bewilderment. 'Yes,' he said, 'and they've gone to Weimar, or as he said, Labassecour.'

Charlotte brightened and straightened herself.

'Do you really think she drew inspiration from me? She didn't even like *Jane Eyre*!'

'No,' said Williams, 'she didn't because your heroine Jane was too conventional when it came to marriage. But *Villette*! That's very different.'

'But no one will speak to them when they return!'

'No one will speak to *her*,' corrected Williams. 'You forget the rules are different for men and women. He'll be able to go about and be accepted. She'll count as his mistress. She will have to stay at home and wait up for him.'

'Dear Heaven,' said Charlotte, signalling to the waiter to bring more coffee. 'Do you think she realises? That's real passion without limits. I don't think that's for Mr Nicholls or me. And you said they can never marry? That's certainly not for me,' she said, blowing her nose, tears or smoke he was not sure which. The coffee arrived and the fire was stoked again. The flames crackled and licked the edges of the inglenook. 'It's comfortable here. Shall we stay for your next example?'

'Who is it?'

'A very dear, complicated man. James Henry Leigh Hunt.'

'I remember I met his daughter at your house. She sang the Italian songs her brother had heard when he lived in Italy with his family at Lord Byron's villa. So pretty, such black, black eyes and a wonderful voice. I was quite overwhelmed, she said she and her brother used to go out and sing in the streets!'

'Indeed they did! The whole family is good looking, musical, literary. Leigh has West Indian blood and all the children are as good looking as he still is. I owe my whole life in literature to him. A man who stood for justice, liberty, and free speech and was imprisoned for it. An extraordinary journalist. When he was publishing *The Examiner* I was just a boy, but I would do anything to lay my hands on an old copy. I hungered after it. How he suffered for his principles. He was accused of libelling the Prince Regent.'

'What did he say?'

'Both the brothers, John and Leigh, were radicals, but monarchists and loyal Englishmen. But they hated injustice, criticising flogging in the army when one thousand lashes had been given; Bonaparte's men, they said, were treated better than our soldiers. Lord Ellenborough thought it would lead to disaffection. Then they were appalled when the King's insanity resulted in the Regency; criticised the Regent for being dissolute, an indebted libertine not worthy of the people, particularly the starving people. Lord E decided it was time to get them; he packed the jury with his own supporters and got the result he wanted, giving them two years each in prison and fines of £500 each.'

'Heavens,' said Charlotte. 'How brave. They must have known the consequences.'

'Yes. Paying off that fine meant that he never had any money for the rest of his life. Children, lodgings, Marianne's problems—'

'Problems,' interrupted Charlotte. 'What problems?'

Williams considered. He looked away, out of the window into the alley, bustling with people, and back again to the fire. His feelings for her made him bold. He looked straight at her, taking her hands in his. Finally he spoke.

'Strictly between ourselves?' he said. 'She drinks.'

Charlotte leant towards him, lowering her voice. 'Poor man,' she said. 'I can't remember if you ever knew about my brother. You know he died, of course, the first of us to go. Emily caught cold at his funeral and never went out again. Branwell drank and it affected all our lives. He took laudanum too to lessen what he felt was the pain of his life. He had no idea of the pain he caused in ours,' she added bitterly.

Williams sensed a great trauma. He remained silent.

'I feel so guilty,' she sighed. 'When he was at his worst I was very hard. It was Emily who lugged him back from the pub, staggering through the churchyard with him vomiting up the path. Anne used to go out with a bucket of water and a broom so that it was clean before the morning. Mr Nicholls would watch from his lodgings in the lane and go out to help Emily. I – I just stayed indoors and tried to block it out. Papa had to sleep with him every night in case he harmed himself.' She blushed. 'Branwell was in love with his employer's wife and she naturally spurned him. How could he be so stupid?' She tried to cancel out this harshness. 'I really loved him when we were children, he was my writing partner in our stories and newspapers and we were so close. I couldn't bear it when he changed into a snivelling, self-pitying drunk...'

Williams was shocked. He had no idea that these sensitive, passionate writers had been involved in the day-to-day misery of living with a drunk. He had met Anne, charming, pretty, shy. The vision of her in the churchyard with the bucket and broom was not a pleasant one, but it accounted for the clarity of her alcoholic character in the *Tenant of Wildfell Hall*. 'Now, now,' said he softly, sensing tears not far off, 'we all do things we regret, but the past is the past.'

She blew her reddened nose on a tiny lace handkerchief. 'I know. But I hated it so much, he was always trying to get money out of the verger for drink, then setting fire to the bed curtains; Em doused the flames, hauled him out and had the whole place back to normal before Papa came back from his meeting. I hated the village gossiping about him. I just railed about it and did nothing.'

'I'm sure you were a support to your sisters—'

'No I wasn't,' she said brutally. 'I just ignored it if I could. Oh, I helped with the odd clean-up because even I couldn't bear to let our dear old servant see the mess he made. But how can Mr Nicholls love me when he saw how badly I behaved towards Branwell, and how I let Papa and Emily and Anne cope on their own?' The tears came now and she did not try to stem them. 'Papa adored him. He was very clever, like Papa; he could do anything, Greek, Latin, turn it all into English verse, play the flute and organ. But he was flawed, brilliant but flawed. So self-indulgent.' She shuddered. 'He never went away to school or university; too fragile, Papa knew it and protected him. But I could have been better to him. It's too late now.'

'Try to forget.' said Williams, realising the enormity of her distress; he rose to his feet and pulled her up with him. Taking her in his arms he hugged her tiny frame to him; she did not resist.

Silent seconds passed ending in a deep sigh as she stopped the tears and came back to the present.

'Tell me about Leigh Hunt,' she whispered. 'I feel I know him a little. There was always sunshine in his work, despite his trials.'

'No need to tell you,' said Williams, releasing her reluctantly from his grasp and replacing the embrace with a more orderly arm link. 'Tomorrow we'll go and see him.'

CHAPTER 14

A Sleepless Night

Williams spent an anxious, sleepless night in Campden Hill: he had left Charlotte in Bedford Square with the promise of the next day's expedition to the Hunts. His house was still, very still despite all the bodies sleeping in it, from Margaret in their bed on the first floor overlooking the lane, to little Anna curled up with older sisters; boys sprawled dreaming of heaven knows what, his two working musical daughters worn out with pupils and house chores, and the very young maid, tucked into her bed at the back of the kitchen. It was for all of them that he had kept the hated job as the bookkeeper at a lithographers, until the joyous day when George Smith came to settle his account and liked his opinions and asked him to work for Smith Elder as their reader and publishing manager.

A beam of moonlight silvered its way towards the stairs where he shed his surtout and hat; his stick nearly slipped from his hand but he caught it deftly before it hit the wooden floor and woke anyone. Suddenly weary, he sat on the second stair, hands round his knees, watching the moonlight illumine the hallway; the cheap prints of the writers he so cherished, the scuff marks where innumerable boots came and went throughout the day, the polished looking glass which had been a wedding present many years ago. How could it be, he wondered, that he, who had so carefully organised his life to support his children and cherish his wife by using the distraction of literature to keep him emotionally fed, how could it be that he was plunged into a vortex of emotion by a little woman with whom he had corresponded for years and met not infrequently to help business along? Was it that he was flattered by her choice of him for advice on her dilemma? Was it a meeting of souls? Whatever caused it had knocked him sideways. Nearly old enough to be her father, his longing to be with her and his pain when he saw her distress was undeniable. And then his feelings towards Mr Nicholls! It was clear she was trying to persuade herself out of loneliness to marry him; Williams groaned at the thought of this stolid Irishman; even her father didn't want her to marry him, and he, according to Charlotte, was literary, imaginative, gifted. He must think the man would bore her rigid. Williams had begun to loathe Nicholls with a vehemence that surprised his gentle soul. He would hardly be an objective adviser. He got up and walked softly up the stairs, pausing to look out of the arched landing window into the garden below, into the Lewes' garden. There was trouble enough there, from extramarital feelings. How could he find himself in this position, a married man with eight children, falling in love with his best novelist? And she, she who seemed to be not unmoved by him?

Arriving at his bedroom door he eased it open and went into the dim room. Margaret always opened the curtains before she went to sleep; she liked to watch the sun come up and be ready for the children, large and small, the moment the movement of the house started. He looked at her sleeping form, clearly outlined in the moonlight. Dear frail, gentle soul; they had been through much together, grown apart as the years went by; she was more intimate with her daughters really than with him, but endlessly patient with him, understanding of the long hours he worked and the extra nights reviewing for *The Spectator* to make ends meet, never reproachful, appreciative of his efforts for the family. She was only mildly critical of the arrangements, as she tentatively called them, next door. Pulling at his stock to loosen it, he wondered what on earth she would think of him being shaken to the core of his emotions by this little woman. Climbing into bed, he considered whether he had become vulnerable because his emotional life these days existed in the fiction he read, analysed, and reviewed. He lay still on his cold side of the bed; his mind was flooded with images of Charlotte.

Her night was equally restless. She loved the anonymity of London and relished the independence she felt in this comfortable room on her own. Getting into the huge bed, her tiny body had almost disappeared into the fine feather mattress, and now she lay on her side watching the changing patterns of light on the curtains as cabs clopped and jingled past, their lamps swaying. But would she have been so content here without Mr Williams – Will – looking after her and listening to her? Did she really want to consider Mr Nicholls? Perhaps Papa was right and he was not the man for her, although she suspected a motive behind his opposition. Mr Nicholls said it was the woman he loved, not the novelist. But she *was* a novelist. Her whole life since she was a tiny child had been bound up with writing, her little books, the newspapers she and her siblings produced from paper scrounged from the kitchen, the poetry her father had written sitting on his shelves. She *was* her books, how could she live with a man who loved the woman, not the novelist? Now Will – he would love the novelist in her, as well as the woman. He of all people understood the travail of writing, the thrills and disappointments, he had found the words to comfort and encourage her as she struggled to publish, he had known the wrestling with words, the struggle to create. But thinking that he would love the novelist in her? What was she thinking? She should not think of him; he was a married man like Monsieur Heger, like Mr Rochester. She had indeed thought of married men before.

Hot and feeling fierce, she released herself from the mattress's embrace and stood by the window, her burning feet cooling on the smooth carpet. Lifting the curtain, she looked out onto the street. It was later now and a young, shabby woman, with the remnants of good looks and obvious intent, loitered across from the house until a well-dressed man appeared round the corner. He hesitated when she approached him, then offered her his arm. They disappeared into the night. *Dear Heaven*, thought Charlotte, *will it always be thus for women, this struggle for existence, always needing men to provide for them, making compromises in order to eat?* She lit the candle and tried to cool her rage, thirstily drinking from the glass by her bed. She had come here to simplify things.

Now they were immeasurably more complicated.

CHAPTER 15

Infinite Riches in a Little Room

Thunder rumbled from the dark skies above Oxford Street but Charlotte was undeterred in her brisk walk towards the omnibus stand. She had arranged to meet Williams there, deflecting his objections to her solitary walk from the boarding house; did he not realise, she had said, that she walked everywhere, that they could never afford to keep a carriage in Haworth? Neither did he realise, she thought, that walking in London fascinated, as well as appalled her. She had never seen the extremes of society before: squalid poverty, dirty diseased children sweeping paths for rich women in the filthy streets, narrow alleys, dark and stinking, close to the fine stone-faced houses of the wealthy. She had even, guiltily curious, peered down Wimpole Street number 50; she knew Elizabeth Barrett and her poet Robert Browning were now safely in Florence in the sunshine, with spaniel and faithful maid, but it still thrilled her to look covertly at the house and imagine the drama that had taken place within, before she eloped with her lover. Lover. She thought suddenly of last evening, and the strength of emotion she had felt when Will had taken her in his arms; to her it had not been fatherly, she loved his smell, his touch, the strength in his hold.

What had he been feeling?

Suddenly the clouds cleared and a watery sun appeared; the piles of manure in the street steamed gently in the new warmth; she could see people waiting for the omnibus going west. She hesitated, screwing up her short-sighted eyes to find a way across the road, between the cabs and buses, trying to avoid the worst of the dirt. A gust of wind tugged at her bonnet; she staggered a little in her attempt to hold onto it. A little boy pulled at her arm on the other side, wanting to sweep her a path across the road; she nodded, and as she followed his sweeping brush she fumbled in her bag for his reward. Before she had reached the other side, she saw Williams's tall figure reach out to the child and hand him something; he touched his greasy urchin cap and disappeared to find more trade.

When Will took her arm in his it seemed the most natural thing in the world. He wore a dark red stock in place of his usual white one; his silk hat shone with brushing. They joined the huddle of people waiting for the bus, every hour bound for Hammersmith. Suddenly it was there, steaming horses, clattering hooves slithering to a halt.

'Let's go upstairs!' she cried, dragging at his arm towards the back where the conductor stood; he protested that women didn't go upstairs, that they would get wet, but she indicated the pale sun and dragged him after her. 'You're a soft southerner,' she called to him as she broke free and made for the knife board seats, back to back, facing outwards. 'We'll see everything from here!'

'You're right,' he replied mildly; he did part of this journey every day on this route and usually preferred to sit inside reading the newspapers provided. But her enthusiasm rejuvenated him, and they were soon settled side by side overlooking the centre of the road. The protocol of the bus, full of respectable passengers who could pay the high fares, seemed to be to ignore everyone else, so that their conversation became more whispered, although most of it was carried away by the wind. Feeling cold, she was glad of Will as a windbreak, not that she would ever admit that it might have been warmer inside. They were still in the busy part of town and he could see her peering down side streets; she had told him she had hardly seen London this way, the way it was now that she was walking, rather than being squired around by George Smith in cabs, as a precious commodity for his business. Although a Tory, her father had been a huge force for good among his poorer parishioners, never failing to visit the tubercular and typhus-ridden houses in the parish, not flinching from cholera when it eventually swept in, giving practical relief despite his small means.

But the destitution and disease of this capital city, renowned for its great wealth and culture! She had been kept well away from it when she visited the Great Exhibition.

'It really is as Dickens says,' she murmured. 'I wish I had written like him to raise public consciousness.'

'You did,' he replied. 'You showed the plight of women on their own, their vulnerability when unprotected and unemployed.'

She wrinkled her eyebrows. 'I suppose I did. But in Haworth we had poor people but no one starved. There are layers beneath this poverty which should never be.' Suddenly the horses started to slow and they were jolted together. The murky streets had given way to greenery, and there were market gardens, washing drying and women in small paddocks milking cows. 'Goodness! What a change in such a short time!' There were single and semi-detached villas being built, and the bus stopped more frequently. Williams hoped they were carrying enough water for the horses, whose life expectancy was short in this gruelling transport work. He put his arm beneath her cloak so that he could hold her tight, a pretence to shield her from the jolting bus. There was no resistance.

'How far is it now?' she said, leaning against him, still intrigued by the changes. 'Why does Leigh Hunt live so far out?'

'In the time I have known him,' said Williams close to her ear, apparently not wanting to spread gossip with the other passengers, 'which is a long time, he has moved at least twenty times. He was last in Kensington in two houses, and as you know he has been in Hampstead several times. We literary hacks,' he coughed slightly, 'we always live on a financial knife edge. I opted for regular, dull employment to have a regular income. Writers are dependent on money being paid for whatever they write; it doesn't always happen, weeks go by without a payment, work dries up. Leigh has moved whenever it seemed he might save a guinea or two on the rent of a different house.'

'So I am lucky to be protected by living in my father's house,' murmured Charlotte.

'Indeed. Ever thought why there are so many women novelists? Sometimes he had to move,' he dropped his voice even more, 'to escape from creditors abused by Marianne. The last address was saddest of all; his youngest son, Vincent, who lived with them, died. He loved him, possibly, more than any of his children although,' and he paused here, thinking, 'that I can hardly believe. Some children are easier than others, but you love them all the same. Anyway,' he continued, 'he couldn't bear the house for the reminders it had of Vincent, so he moved again, this time to Hammersmith, near his daughter Jacintha.' Suddenly the axle took a dive into a huge rut and the horses stopped. They heard the driver encouraging them to go on. 'You will find his present home a cottage. He's happy in it. Everywhere he goes he creates a study, almost a bower, full of books and flowers and busts of his favourite writers. He's resilient, brave, loyal, and charming. A little improvident; but you'll love him.'

The bus slowed again, stopping near Cornwall Road. They clambered down the stairs quickly before it lumbered off again towards the Broadway. Charlotte's grip on his arm was vicelike, her face white with anxiety. She'd always found meeting people, especially in London, difficult: their expectations, her fears. Williams stopped at the end of the road, and turned to her.

'Of all the people you might meet,' he said reassuringly, 'this man is the easiest, the kindest you could possibly encounter. Remember how the *Examiner* praised *Jane Eyre;* all his life he has championed new writers and recognised talent.'

'Like you,' said Charlotte.

'No,' he said firmly. 'He has a touch of genius as well as a brave conscience. You are going to see a man who has known, loved, and helped Shelley and Keats, and was lauded by Byron.'

Charlotte gulped. They were walking past neat terraced cottages, still surrounded by fields.

'If you put it like that, I should be terrified.'

He took his arm out of hers as they turned in at a small iron gate, rapping the solid wooden door with his stick. It was very quiet. A hand was scrabbling with the lock and a tall, elegant old man appeared, wrapped in a duster coat with a black silk cape; white hair abundant, eyebrows still dark, large intelligent dark eyes flooding with pleasure at the sight of Will. He peered closely at Charlotte.

'And this – is Miss Brontë?' His voice was low, beautiful. 'Come in, come in!'

They followed him into a narrow hall, and then into the front of the two ground floor parlours. There were French windows at either end, the back looking over a pretty winter garden and the front into the lane and then across to market gardens. The furniture, desperately in need of care, was grey with dust and not a little rickety. He settled Charlotte onto a thinly padded chair near his writing table, where books and flowers mingled together riotously. More flowers stood in jars around the room. Busts of poets leaned down perilously upon them from shelves and small plinths.

'Will is one of my dearest, oldest friends,' he said to her, his black eyes sparkling. 'Almost the only one who regularly visits me now that I live so far out.' There was a crash from upstairs, something hard hitting the wooden floor, then rolling. They all ignored it. 'I hardly go out now, the streets are dangerous with the whirling omnibuses—'

'Which nevertheless bring us to see you—'

'—and I prefer to read my books again and see my children who live near.' The article above rolled back to where it had come from. 'Would you like some tea? I drink a lot of good dark tea, nothing green.' He went to the door and as he opened it a scruffy young maid was disappearing up the stairs.

'Molly, some tea for my friends, please,' he said amiably.

'I'm seeing to Missus,' was the reply as the dirty pinafore vanished.

Leigh sighed. 'It will come soon,' he said mildly. 'Miss Brontë, we are so lucky to have our little servant.' She had looked quite big to Charlotte. 'Will and my other friends were good enough to petition for a civil list pension for me, otherwise I might be destitute!' He laughed. 'Mostly I now enjoy the beatitude of paying as I go and incurring no more debts. Although recently...' He glanced to the ceiling. Will hastily filled in.

'Mrs Hunt needs medical attention,' he said pointedly to Charlotte. *I bet she does,* thought Charlotte, *just like Branwell, bottles and bottles of it.* The front door clicked then banged shut. The parlour door was pushed open. A beautiful young woman, clad in lavender, pink, and a dash of scarlet, came in.

'It's Miss Brontë, isn't it?' she sparkled. 'Hello, Will. I last saw Miss Brontë at your house on her first visit to London.'

Leigh interrupted. 'This is my daughter Julia. She's a dear girl, but will not take life seriously.' He frowned meaningfully at her as if to stem further spontaneity.

'No point, is there Miss Brontë? Are you still shackled to the family home and burdened with your virginity, living with your father, like me?' Her father raised his hands in despair, Will laughed out loud and Charlotte chuckled. She was a remarkable-looking girl, dark, fine boned, beautiful hair and perfect teeth, small, with a singer's posture. She flopped down on an unsafe chair. 'Have I embarrassed you? I shouldn't say what I think. It's really inconvenient for those who would prefer not to know it!' Molly came heavily down the stairs and knocked peremptorily at the door.

'Missus says she'd like some company. It's either your tea or her company.'

'Get the tea, Molly, please,' said Julia wearily. 'I'll go up.'

Charlotte hesitated, then said, 'Shall I come with you?'

Leigh looked wary and Will said quickly, 'She knows something of the problem.'

Julia smiled. 'Come on, Charlotte. She'll really love seeing you. She loves literary people. She adored Shelley and he her. Keats was passing fond too, despite our noisy house. Follow me.' On this recommendation Charlotte nodded to Will and joined the fascinating Julia.

They mounted the bare wooden staircase. In the dark of winter they needed the single candle Julia had taken off the maid. It flickered on the bare walls, damp patches rendering artistic licence to whorls like sea monsters. Along the landing walls were framed silhouettes. Charlotte stopped and peered at then in the dim light.

'Mama's,' said Julia. 'She was the best cutter of profiles in her day. This is Keats, and that Byron,' Charlotte looked closer, 'and that is Father, bowed down by work. The painter Wilkie said it was impossible to believe that hard scissors could treat the lips with so much expression. She was a sculptress too, she did a bust of Shelley which startled by its likeness.'

There was another candle on the landing, casting faint light into the front bedroom; following Julia, Charlotte could see in the gloom a single curtained bed with a lantern perched on a chest of drawers, well away from the invalid and a fire risk. In the bed loomed a large woman, her face in the cast of Julia but marred by age, weight, and drink. The room was tolerably fragrant, rescued by the strong smell of spirits.

Julia bent down and picked up a brandy bottle that was rolling around on the floor.

'Empty again?' she said, holding it up in the dim light. 'You really are very naughty, Mama, to tell Papa the doctor had prescribed a bottle a day. He believes anything you say! This,' she said, guiding Charlotte nearer to the bed, 'is Miss Brontë.'

'What a pleasure!' The voice was strong, eager. 'I get so little company here, now that I can barely leave the bed for rheumatism. To have a writer like you is like the old days!' Charlotte moved nearer, daringly took the gnarled and slightly grubby hand that lay on the sheet. It was grasped firmly. Julia stood back.

'I loved your first book,' continued Mrs Hunt. 'I think you took Byron for your model of Mr Rochester. You had it right too, Byron cared only for himself but was greatly attractive to women. Not to me of course, I could see right through him and he hated me for that. We had a time of it, a terrible journey to Italy and not much of a welcome except from the Shelleys, and you know what happened to him.' Her voice trembled. 'We were all heartbroken,' and tears started to flow. Julia intervened.

'That's enough, Ma,' she said softly. To Charlotte she breathed quietly, 'She gets upset, particularly after a bottle of brandy.' Tears came to her eyes too. 'Despite the present appearance she's been devoted to my father and to us too. Do you ever think, Charlotte, that the lives of women who appear to have security can be desperately difficult? It's not just lone women struggling to survive, as you write about. Mama had ten children, struggled with Papa's uncertain income to keep us all fed and clothed and educated; the reputation she has gained for fecklessness was no more than necessity, borrowing here and there, forgetting to return. Once married and into annual pregnancies women can be driven mad by anxiety, then laudanum and drink become the only comfort. Dear old Will downstairs is one of the best, he did a dull job for years but kept Margaret sane and happy. A bit of a saint.' She looked hard at Charlotte. 'Are you staying with him?'

'No,' Charlotte replied vaguely, trying to take all this in. Julia was clearly a woman of the world. Momentarily she reflected on her suitability for inclusion in a novel. She must think about that phrase – 'burdened by your virginity'. What an extraordinary girl. They proceeded to entertain Marianne Hunt.

***

Downstairs in the parlour Leigh was tending a meagre fire, his loose cotton garment flapping dangerously near it. Occasionally the few embers glowed, and he reached then for a small bellows and eagerly fanned it into tiny flames. He stirred a little pan of porridge which was beginning to bubble slightly.

'Would you like some?' he asked Will, who shook his head. 'I feed myself mostly, I try to get Molly to concentrate on Marianne's needs, so with nectarines and apples and a few plums I do very well. Julia is a dear girl but often out. She and her brother Henry sing in the streets sometimes, they have beautiful voices and people ask them into their houses and to dinner, then they sing some more.' He paused. 'I don't know if they should do it, but it seems to be fun for them, and they make a little money.'

Will said, 'Last time she came to my house she sang some Italian airs which she heard when you were in Italy—'

'No,' said Leigh, 'she wasn't born until after we returned from Italy. Henry would have heard them and taught her, he had a quick ear as a child.' He sighed. 'She says she will never marry, she doesn't want children and their needs. Can you imagine not wanting children, Will?'

'I can imagine a woman not wanting them. They become worn out with the births, the ensuing medical problems and the chores.'

"Will."

"Yes?"

'Miss Brontë – you and she seem very – intimate – it's the way she looks at you...'

Oh dear, thought Will, *if anyone is going to pick up that I love Miss Brontë it will be this sensitive, affectionate old man.*

'It's the way she looks at you,' Hunt repeated, 'and the way you protect her. You're both as bad as each other, if you understand my meaning. I have to say I am surprised, after all these years of rectitude. You've been as faithful as I have. My only flirtations have been with the eyes.'

'That's what this is,' said Will defensively. 'Miss Brontë needs a little help and support at the moment and I am the right man to do it.' Leigh raised his eyes to the ceiling and chuckled. The porridge bubbled with a sucking sound. The old man removed it from the fire and placed a kettle there instead, possibly thinking he would make the tea himself eventually. 'Thornton is not like you, Will,' he said, gazing at the newly burning flames which softened the shabby appearance of the room, rendering it almost cosy. 'He has provided me with grandchildren from at least two ladies. It's quite difficult at Christmas! I think he absorbed the irregularities of Byron and Shelley when we were in Italy; our own somewhat pedestrian marriage seemed less attractive to him. And he was with me when I was in prison. Sometimes I feel it was wrong to follow my conscience and the literary stars, wrong for my family.'

At this pensive moment Julia and Charlotte came in. Will saw Leigh glance sharply at Charlotte, then he sat her next to him. 'Will and I were just talking about Thornton and his unusual arrangements, which, I must say, result in the loveliest children.' He smiled engagingly. 'Marriage, as Julia will tell you,' he said, signalling to her to stay; lacking a steady chair she sat on the floor by the fire, her fine head silhouetted against the firelight. 'Marriage is not for everyone. I know you approve of it, Miss Brontë, for poor Jane Eyre suffered rather than abuse the sanctity—'

'That,' said Julia with considerable firmness, 'was in her first book. Have you changed your mind since, Charlotte?'

Charlotte was astonished at the directness of this lovely girl. Her questions, in front of Will, made it hard for her to reply. How could she say that, if Will had offered her now the position of his mistress, as Mr Rochester had offered Jane Eyre, after the discovery of his wife incarcerated in the attic, she would have gladly accepted? She looked across the room at his fire-lit profile and knew she could not be without him. Aloud, she said to Julia: 'I think I am a little more tolerant, a little less firm in my views now. *Jane Eyre* was very black and white. Now I know that men and women fall in love without intending to and can find their hearts broken by it.'

There was silence, interrupted only by the soft rumbling of the kettle, shifting on the fire. Leigh

Hunt, sensing deep thoughts in all the people in the room, said, 'You are right. Let me tell you about Shelley and his loves, and Byron and his. They were both married, and as you say, fell in love afterwards and broke hearts other than their own. I'll tell you about Italy, where Marianne and I went with our six – then – children. And Shelley's death, and Mary's broken heart. And Harriet's. And Claire's.' Charlotte's eyes grew large. He piled coal on the fire generously, profligately. 'We need to be warm. It's a long story.' She moved to sit by Julia on the floor, settling her back against Will's knees, arms around her own.

Julia laughed, reaching for a tattered cushion to soften the bare boards she was sitting on. 'You'll scarcely believe this, Charlotte,' she said, 'but he tells it very well, but then, he was the best journalist of his time!'

From upstairs a voice called: 'Open the door wide! I want to hear it again!' Hunt, being nearest, stood up and stopped the door open with a pile of books. Darkness had fallen outside, and rain was pattering against the long windows; they settled expectantly.

CHAPTER 16

Mr Hunt's Italian Journey

1822

Hunt braced himself on the thin mattress as the ship rolled, pitched, then rolled again. A child had crawled from its bunk – in the dark he wasn't sure which one but it was a small, young one – and was nestled in close to his body, smelling faintly of vomit. However hard he tried it was impossible to keep them clean. Marianne lay close by but at night she slept deeply, for which he was thankful, for her days were torture to her, and he lived daily with the prospect of losing her. When she spat blood he feared that she had tuberculosis, picked up from Keats when he stayed with them in Hampstead; doctors diagnosed differently and kept bleeding her. Shelley had advised a sea passage instead of the rigours of the road; he was fond of Marianne and she adored him, mothered him, accepted anything he said. Hunt shut his eyes against the darkness and wondered if the whole expedition had been a mistake; six children, a servant girl, an ailing wife; another huge wave crashed and sent the boat spinning, heaving, the cargo booming and rattling below.

Cargo. He had been horrified to find that along with the sugar there was a consignment of gunpowder bound for the rebels in Greece; Marianne was terrified every time the drunk cook appeared in their cabin with a lantern to access provisions in the hold, fearful he would blow up the little ship as he lurched unsteadily, the flame at risk from his trembling hand. But once they were there, and seeing Shelley again! He eased himself off the mattress, tucking the sleeping child closer to Marianne, and cautiously made his way up to the deck, remembering to duck as he reached the top of the ladder. He was a tall man, slender and willowy, his dark skin roughened by the constant beating of the wind; the wind blew his long dark hair and he had tied it in a pigtail, which gave him an unintentionally nautical air. It was just becoming light, a magical time as the horizon appeared mistily and a pale sun fought with clouds. Even with the storm raging the sun came up.

The ship was quiet at this hour, apart from the endless screaming of the wind and the plaintive quacking of a few caged ducks who were constantly soaked by sea water; they could hardly survive long. Holding the rigging tightly he gingerly moved towards the tethered goat which had been brought aboard to provide fresh milk for the children; the poor creature's fear had dried up her milk and she now lay in a little bed she had made for herself on a piece of canvas, where she lay shivering, intermittently soaked by breaking waves. He slipped on the poor creature's dung then bent down to caress the small white head. Suddenly he sensed a little figure behind him.

'Thornton? You must be careful, my boy, I told all of you not to come on deck when it was rough and dark.' The boat hit another wave with a tremendous crash and Leigh grabbed him.

'I'm older than the others, Papa! I came for the goat. Can we take her into the cabin? She's so frightened, I can't bear to think of her up here on her own. And the ducks—'

Leigh considered as he tried to brace the child against some rigging and cover him with his body. The shrieking wind made it nearly impossible to think. He agreed with his son, but how to get the animal down the narrow ladder? The ducks were out of the question, they would cause too much disruption flapping about, but the goat might just bed down with the rest of them. 'If I try to hold her body,' he shouted to Thornton above the wind, 'and you just guide the legs, we might make it down the ladder.' The creature didn't mind at all being picked up, it was the sea that terrified her, not people, and very slowly they managed to move their furry burden into the cabin. It was now lighter and the children were stirring, moving around in their bunks. Five pairs of merry black eyes stared and the baby clapped his hands with joy. Marianne swore softly.

'What are you thinking of? There's not enough space for us let alone the goat! And it's bad enough every time a chamber pot spills in the storm, and now you want the goat to pee everywhere!'

'Please, Mama!' A chorus, orchestrated with raised hands by Thornton from behind Marianne, joyfully pleaded from the bunks as dark tousled heads peered out. Even Elizabeth the servant smiled.

'What a family you are!' she croaked, hoarse from sea sickness. 'I never did see the like!'

'My dear,' began Leigh persuasively, 'if the goat is with us and less frightened she may produce milk. Think of that!'

'Yes, yes!' cried the children, 'think of that Mama!'

Marianne smiled, rare on this expedition. She could never resist her husband or her children. They were overwhelmingly the reason for her being. She raised her hands in surrender and busied herself with the baby and nappies which she hung above the smoking fire. The goat settled peacefully by the fire, head on hooves, warming up for the first time in days. John and Henry joined Thornton and nestled up to her warm flanks.

The storm continued to rage. They were constantly being beaten back up the Channel, making no headway, but never put into a port as that incurred charges. So the interminable pitch and toss, the soaking of the waves on deck and then spewing down into the cabin, the whistling, moaning wind, the constant sickness, left them all exhausted. Leigh was never sick, and that left him free to look after all of them, and besides the mopping up and cleaning and clothes washing, he kept the children's spirits up with stories and songs, so they never complained, in fact they looked upon it as the adventure he had intended it to be. Not so Marianne: her sickness and her coughing was making her more and more vulnerable. Seeing them happy with their new friend the goat, to whom they were now feeding the remaining sweet biscuits, he slipped away to the deck again.

Bracing himself against the wind, he slithered his way crablike towards the wheel where two figures rhythmically bent to the soaking the waves gave them. The mate, Mr Transom, had fought with Nelson at Trafalgar so had all the qualities of a Royal Navy man. After the war, like so many heroic men, he had fallen on hard times and was glad to accept a cargo ship. Although the brig needed a large crew to sail her, most of them were below either sick or tired and the seaman on watch was dangerously near to sleep. Transom took the wheel from the young man and bid him go below. After a mountainous wave almost knocked them off their feet, Transom said, 'Never seen weather like this, Mr Hunt, in thirty years at sea. This storm is in its fiftieth hour! Why did you choose to sail in December?'

'Choose I did not,' replied Hunt, 'we aimed for September but the delay over the cargo meant a late departure. I would never have chosen this for my wife and children.'

Transom was a burly man with craggy good looks and sensitive blue eyes hidden among wiry eyebrows.

'Your oldest – Thornton is it? – seems happy enough. I found him in the longboat with the goat, whittling a piece of wood into a cutlass to go with his pirate clothes.' He chuckled. 'Perhaps he'll be a sailor.' Hunt looked at the sky as blue lightning crackled and rent it into terrifying light. He fervently hoped not. 'You're bound for Italy you said? What takes you there?' He grasped the wheel harder and leaned over to take the huge swell.

'Indeed. I have good friends who have invited me to join them in publishing a periodical in England which we will edit from Italy. It seemed such an opportunity, the country, the warm weather,' he looked ruefully around, 'the hope that our work would go some way to changing the world, the company of poets...'

'Poets indeed!' shouted Mr Transom. 'I like a bit of poetry. Lord Nelson was a reading man, and the Navy is full of songs and dances! I wish this lot were more lively! What poets would you be going to, Mr Hunt?'

Hunt grabbed the rigging as another mountain of water heaved towards them, flecked with windblown spume. 'Lord Byron and Mr Percy Shelley,' he shouted hoarsely, unable to keep the pride out of his voice. 'Do you know of them?'

Transom laughed. 'Who hasn't heard of Lord Byron? If you haven't read the poems you've heard about the life. What these people get up to! Most men can't feed their families and they're spending money like water on the ladies and high living. If you can read a newspaper you know all about it. Just as well most men can't read or there'd be a revolution like in France!'

Hunt was inclined to agree with the broad sentiment but felt the need to defend poets. 'I grant you Lord Byron has a colourful life, but a most remarkable pen. But I think you would, according to your last remarks, like Mr Shelley greatly. He embraces better conditions for the poor, involves himself in poor relief, even plans revolution. He believes in free love...'

'Free love!' chortled the First Mate. 'Whatever is free about love once you're married! I notice you have Mrs Hunt and your brood with you, and I have mine on land, I see them about twice a year or less in this job. But I'm not free.' He bent at an acute angle to pull the wheel back as he steered into the quickening storm, then let it roll back through his frozen hands. The Captain appeared, pulling himself along by lurching from the base of various riggings to reach them. He then had to pause to get his breath.

'I'll take an hour, Mr Transom,' he shouted. 'You go below; I need to think about what we do next. We can't go on like this, so many of the crew sick and no sign of this storm going away.' He glanced at Hunt. 'You're all right, sir?'

'I'm well, but I am worried for my wife and the children. Not this one,' he continued, as he caught sight of Thornton swinging towards them on the rigging.

'Papa,' he shouted, 'it's easier if you swing from rope to rope rather than stumble along the deck!'

'Not a choice I have,' laughed Hunt, 'come here and stay with me.'

Transom said to him, 'I'm going to my cabin for an hour. Care to join me – and the lad? Step to then.'

They struggled behind him to his tiny cabin, tucked under the mainsail. Despite its size and lack of height, it was clean and warm, lit by a single candle firmly defended in a latticed lantern. Nowhere on the ship was dry; in the crew's quarters hammocks bulbous with seaman were suspended and stale food and buckets of vomit and worse stood unemptied by a crew devastated by sickness and disease; the sea swilled around with every outsize wave. Thornton leapt joyfully into Mr Transom's hammock and set it swaying; Transom pointed Hunt to a galleried chair while he himself perched against the wall. He produced a flask and handed it to Hunt, who took a small sip. Thornton's hand stretched out from the hammock towards the flask and was pushed back by his father.

'So this free love,' said Transom, 'how does that work out?'

Hunt locked his hands in front of him, musing on their dirty chapped state. 'In Shelley's case he felt that no human being had the right to possess another, even in marriage, which was a legal arrangement made for the sake of land and children.' He sounded unconvinced. 'Shelley had a wife, Harriet, but he met the daughter, Mary, of two philosophers, Mary Wollstonecraft and William Godwin. Not only was he enraptured by her beauty, but also her parentage! They were anarchists and radicals. Mary was only sixteen, but equally enraptured by Shelley and they ran away with her stepsister, Claire, to Europe. Mary soon had children by Shelley. Mary's other stepsister, left alone to look after William Godwin, took an overdose and died. Shelley's wife drowned herself, leaving two small children—'

'Sink me!' said the First Mate. 'It sounds like trouble!'

'It was,' replied Hunt. 'They were so very young, racketing around Europe, the girls pregnant and

Shelley distracted from writing by the practicalities of living. After Harriet drowned herself, Shelley and Mary married—'

'Married? Why? I thought he didn't believe in marriage?'

'Lord knows,' sighed Hunt sadly. 'But by the time she was twenty-one she had lost three children and fell into a dreadful depression. Shelley was fighting for custody of his children, which Harriet's parents opposed. It was not a happy time. Claire, Mary's stepsister, had a daughter by Byron. Now that was unusual. She decided she too wanted a poet, and more or less,' he glanced at the still hammock and coughed slightly, 'seduced Byron, who,' he coughed again glancing at the hammock, 'responded. Their child Allegra is four years old and in a convent.'

'At least she's tucked away safely,' laughed Transom. 'Although you never know what goes on these days.'

'There was also a baby in Naples who Shelley registered; no one knew if it was his.'

The hammock stirred. 'Shall I meet all these people when we get to Italy, Papa? They sound really interesting.'

'I thought you were asleep!' exclaimed Hunt. 'Yes, you will but you won't talk about it. Forget you ever heard it.'

A crash shook the boat to its guts. Water coursed down the ladder despite the closed door to the cabin. It opened and the captain's head appeared. 'Come up, Transom,' he shouted. 'We'll have to find a harbour. We can't continue like this.' As if endorsing him the rushing water almost pitched him down the steps.

'Aye aye, sir,' shouted Transom, and disappeared.

***

Hunt felt he had seldom been so happy. Looking around the ship skimming gently through the clear sea, he laughed as his six children swarmed across the deck, barefoot, sunburnt in their tattered clothes. His joyous reunion with Shelley hovered in his mind continually. Marianne sat on a pile of coiled ropes attempting to mend a shredded shirt; her muslin frock, fluttering in the warm breeze, had faded to an indeterminate colour and revealed her stout ankles and plump arms. He went to sit beside her.

'All right?' he asked fondly.

'Indeed!' she replied. 'Sometimes I can't believe we survived that journey in December. Look at them now.' She shaded her eyes with her hand and smiled. 'They're so well and happy.'

Hunt leaned against her and took her hand. 'I wish you were better,' he said softly, 'I thought I would lose you. How could I have borne that? And all that time you were so terribly ill you never complained. The relief when we put into Plymouth in that storm! But it was pleasant, was it not, the way the people there welcomed us, knowing that I was the editor of the *Examiner*?'

Marianne smiled proudly. 'What a presentation they gave you, that lovely silver cup. How well they think of you! That encouragement started you writing again.'

'Our only problem,' replied Hunt ruminatively,

catching Mary Florimel as she hurtled past, nearly naked, plump brown body burnished by the sun, and sitting her on his knee, 'is the debt we now have from five months lodging in Devon as well as the new sea passage and losing our first booking. Byron put up the money for the voyage. I hope he will reimburse for the delay through the expenses for the *Liberal*. We're also six months behind our expected arrival time which may have inconvenienced our hosts.'

Thornton, suspended over the side a little way off with a stick and something bent on the end of it, ears open, shouted, 'Shall I see Mr Shelley when we arrive? I liked him when he was in Hampstead with us. He was good for games.' He had been fascinated by grampuses and dolphins on this part of the voyage, and silver fish, as his father said, falling into the water like a sprinkle of shillings.

They were expecting Shelley to meet them at Leghorn, and accompany them to Pisa where the lower floor of Byron's Palazzo Lanfranchi had been prepared for them. Marianne dreaded the meeting with Byron; they had never been on good terms, whereas she adored both the Shelleys. He anticipated a few problems there: Byron was not known for his tolerance, neither was Marianne, except for her own family. Hunt put the child back on her feet and leaned over the side, peering into the startlingly transparent turquoise water. The sun was hot on his back, his dark American skin, he felt, made him a natural heat worshipper. He shrugged, putting possible conflict out of his mind, thrilled by the approaching shimmering coastline, white dwellings, pantiled roofs, colourful awnings, blue water, blue sky, sails of every colour, a new life, new writing, his children all around; what more could a man want?

In the noise of disembarkation Leigh tried to see Shelley; his height would distinguish him among the smaller jostling Italians, just as Hunt would be distinguished by the children bubbling around him, as well as the goat, a steadfast survivor who was still with them. Settling his wide-brimmed straw hat on his head, he picked up Henry and put him on his shoulders to prevent trampling. Suddenly he heard his name.

'Is that Mr Hunt?' called an English voice. 'Mr Leigh Hunt?'

'Indeed it is,' cried Hunt, trying to identify the voice in the babel of languages. Thornton appeared (Hunt had not realised he had disappeared) pulling a handsome bronzed man by the cuff.

'Papa,' said Thornton, man to man, 'this is Mr Trelawney, I was just looking at his boat.'

Trelawney cuffed him good naturedly round the ear. 'He was actually below deck with the boatswain. Quite a curious lad, isn't he? Are you his father? You have your hands full. I'm Edward Trelawney, here in place of Shelley, with Lord Byron's boat, Bolivar. Shelley is delayed, he's had some domestic difficulties, but he'll be here soon.' Trelawney was a veritable *Corsair*. He had come to Italy from Cornwall in pursuit of the Byron myth, fast gathering adherents all over Europe, and even looked as Hunt remembered Byron, tall, vibrant, and romantic.

Hunt untangled Henry from his shoulders. 'I'll have to make arrangements for my wife and the other children,' Trelawney winced, 'and then I'll be with you.' His heart sank at the news of Shelley's domestic difficulties. On their multiple journeys across Europe the Shelleys had endured bad carriages, long walks through mountainous territory, and hunger when money didn't arrive from England. They had lost and miscarried children in the extremes of heat and cold. For Mary, the grief for the children was compounded by her volatile feelings at Harriet Shelley's suicide, which allowed her to marry Shelley, and hard on that her own unhappy stepsister Fanny's overdose and death. She had just miscarried a child at Lerici, their summer house along the coast from Leghorn, becoming ill, depressed, and anxious by Shelley's seeming indifference. All this between the ages of sixteen and twenty-one. The sweetness of Shelley's character was sometimes overwhelmed by his passions: ideas, women, boats. Trelawney said Byron had suggested that before going on to Pisa Hunt should take a carriage out to his summer house at Montenero. He had one waiting.

Leaving the children and Octavia the goat, renamed monthly according to how long she had been with them, at an inn, Hunt bowled along the dusty suburban roads in a creaking carriage into the countryside, dark blue hills framing the baking landscape. Thornton had somehow managed to catch the tail board of the carriage and then swung himself dustily inside. Trelawney sighed as Hunt mildly welcomed him aboard. He warned Hunt that Lord Byron's daughter Allegra had recently died in the convent he had sent her to. 'He never sees his legitimate daughter Ada,' added Trelawney, 'so tread carefully.'

Is there no end to this grief? thought Hunt. All spilling from love gone wrong and broken hearts, new loves leaving children in their wake.

In the Villa Rossi, named according to its ruddy colour, Lord Byron welcomed him them cordially, and drew him into the house where his mistress, Teresa Giuiccoli, wept over the injury to her brother, stabbed in a fracas among the servants. *This*, thought Hunt, *is real Latin living!* Byron, whom he had not seen for four years, was much changed; the slim, athletic young man with shiny dark curls and clear-cut features had become bloated and fat, his hair dressed in greasy ringlets. But there was no doubting the warmth of his greeting. He remembered Hunt's kindness when Lady Byron had left him among dark rumours of his unnatural behaviour, and said so.

'You extended the kindness to Shelley too, did you not?' said His Lordship. 'Protecting us in the hour of need from clinging women. But you seem to have a stable situation yourself,' he continued, eyeing Thornton with languorous dislike, watching the child exploring his exotic artefacts and examining the cranes, falcons, and crows perched on various huge potted eucalyptus and palms. Thornton kept well clear of the hound whose throat rumblings were designed to repel him, but sensing the noble Lord's hostility he disappeared to the stables where he was soon conducting lively enquiries in his developing Italian, leaving his father to discuss the future of the *Liberal*. It was to be published by Hunt's brother John, although John Murray wanted it badly, and there had been an approach by Keats's publisher Taylor and Hessey. A young Mr Williams, who knew Keats, had written on behalf of John Taylor.

Rumbling back to the city with Thornton asleep across him, Hunt asked Trelawney if he thought Lord Byron was in funds and would be approachable for an advance of some sort.

'He's always in funds,' the young man replied. 'But maybe the answer is no to your question. For a boat and all that goes with it, yes. Otherwise it's unpredictable – he even quibbled about Allegra's funeral costs, arguing that her size should make it a third of the normal price.' Despite the heat and the sweat-soaked shirt clinging to his body, Hunt shivered.

Shelley arrived at Leghorn the next day; tall, freckled, and bony, his haggard look surprised the Hunts. The two men had a euphoric day, wandering arm in arm through the town, drinking deep draughts of the local wine when they sat with Marianne and the children beneath wide coloured awnings shading them from the midday sun.

'It's so hospitable here,' said Hunt enthusiastically, raising his glass to watch the red bubbles chase each other along the rim. 'If we'd been in England the children would not have been welcome.' They certainly were here: their dark skin and hair and bright black eyes endeared them to their Italian hosts, who plied them with strange foods and ignored their roving natures. A shadow passed across Shelley's face.

'Your children seem to thrive here,' he said sadly. 'That is not the case with ours or Byron's.'

'I'm sorry,' said Hunt hastily. 'I should have thought, I...' His voice trailed off, as he realised how the spectacle of his thriving brood must have stopped the hearts of the bereaved parents. Even Byron, a neglectful father, would feel grief as Thornton rocketed around the Casa Rossi delighting in the animals and birds.

Shelley stood up and stooping, kissed Marianne's hand. 'We'll welcome you to Pisa tomorrow.'

The move into the Palazzo Lanfranchi on the lung' Arno produced violently differing emotions. Marianne and Lord Byron, having glanced thunderously at each other, parted, she to bed, he to his upper chambers. The children ran, jumped, and danced through the spacious shady rooms, discovered Byron's garden and sang loudly, with massive gestures, in imitation of the servants. Hunt worked hard to settle his study; the flowers he loved occurred naturally, orange trees framing the windows, and the garden outside penetrating with light which changed from green to fiery copper throughout the day. He felt he had come home, in this beautiful land with its intensity of colour and warmth. But he was also tremulous, uneasy, as if his happiness was fragile; he constantly remembered the deaths of the Shelley and Byron children, the desolate sadness of Mary Shelley at Lerici, and regarded his own rampaging brood with a mixture of love and apprehension.

He was watching the goat, Octavia. She stood contentedly cropping fresh grass, her first for months, in the garden. *You have to admire that goat,* he thought. *She deserves a poem, having survived the journey and now a bitten ear from Byron's guard dog.* Thornton was nippier but still had narrowly avoided the snappy jaws. He heard Shelley calling to the children as he took the wide stone stairs three as a time into the basement.

Reaching Hunt's study he stopped, amazed at the signs of organised industry.

'I'm keen to get on with the *Liberal*,' said Hunt. 'I sense I need to fire up Byron again with this project. Our late arrival has left him a little cold about it.' Shelley nodded. 'It's the only means of support I have in this country, so I need to get on.'

Shelley sat on the stone seat moulded into the window and passed his hat from hand to hand. He dropped his voice and looked straight at Hunt. 'I'm trying to be sure that you and Byron are together on this.' He spoke in a whisper now. 'He certainly did want to do it and he's an honourable man. But you need to be careful; sometimes he thinks you are not respectful enough – you call him Byron and forget the title. Your reputation as a radical and liberal should make him expect this, as would I, but to him it really matters. If you could just remember always to give him his title, whether in writing or conversation, and perhaps make the children a bit less intrusive and noisy?'

Hunt jumped from his chair in a rare display of anger, his black eyes glittering. 'I certainly will do as you say, if it's necessary. My children's robustness is a matter I have constantly been aware of in the shadow of both your losses. But if only he would talk to my wife – he completely ignores her; he drives her to sarcasm and depression. It hurts me deeply, but my position in his house prevents me from challenging him.' He banged his fists on his paper-strewn table and looked out at the idyllic scene outside; such sunlit beauty with subterranean rumblings.

Shelley rested his hand on his shoulder. 'It grieves me too to see how he treats Marianne; she's volatile but the best friend Mary and I have had over the years. I'll try to speak to him but I have to leave here tomorrow.'

Hunt was startled. 'You're going?'

Shelley's face darkened; the lines from nose to mouth were so much deeper than before and beneath his healthy sunburn there was a tense whiteness. 'Yes. Mary is still distressed after the last miscarriage. It was very bad.' He paused, moved across to a shadier part of the room, where his face became hidden in the shadows. 'I've had a foolish flirtation with Jane Williams, Edward's wife, they share the house with us... it's not important, I wrote her a few poems, you know how you do...'

'No,' said Hunt firmly, 'I am very careful about writing poems to women.'

Shelley looked ashamed. 'But it upset Mary.'

Dear Lord, thought Hunt, *not more troubles. I thought these two were soulmates, bound by ideals of freedom and revolution, not to mention 'Frankenstein' which Shelley had edited so successfully.*

'My boat is now finished and Edward has come from Lerici to sail it back with me, she's getting very insistent. I have to go, I don't want her to become unstable...' His voice trailed away.

Hunt felt a ghastly desolation at the young poet's troubled soul. Night had at last fallen, the moon risen above the trees and the loveliness enveloped them, the fragrance of blossoms, the murmuring of animals in Byron's apartment and the clicking of cicadas. Far off, thunder rumbled. Shelley had moved towards the bookcase and, lighting a candle, was now peering closely at the books Hunt had brought with him. He turned and the candle illumined his ravaged face.

'May I borrow the Keats?' he asked softly. He had been deeply affected by the poet's death in Rome the year before, and had written one of his finest poems in his memory. 'Of course I'll return it.'

Hunt spread his hands in acceptance. 'Take whatever you like,' he said. Anything to ease the young man's sadness. Shelley gave him a surprising smile, affectionately squeezed both shoulders in his bony hands, and ran up the stairs. That was the last time Hunt saw him.

***

The day had dawned without the coolness which precedes Leghorn's hottest days. It had felt like a cauldron all night, and thunder rumbled around the hills; rain had fallen heavily then stopped, the streams which rushed down the hills splashed towards the bay, sparkling in the sun. The *Don Juan,* which had been christened *Ariel* by Mary Shelley, had been obstinately renamed by Byron in his own poem's honour. There was friction there. Shelley sailed with Edward Williams, friction there too, and desperate to return to relieve Mary's anxiety, had plunged into stormy seas. Mary and Jane, waiting in the Casa Magni at Lerici, waited in vain. The bodies of the sailors were washed up after a week, fully clothed but ravenously eaten by fishes and buffeted by the storm. Keats's poems were in Shelley's pocket.

***

Hunt was devastated by grief, hardly knowing how to get through the day in his anguish. He tried to comfort his own family and Shelley's; Marianne stayed in bed and wept; Thornton sobbed as only a child can, for he had loved Shelley most of his life, their unorthodox spirits mingling in joy and sadness. The other children were less comprehending and Hunt tried to keep them so. Byron was stunned and cold: his differences with the dead poet before he died filled him with remorse, and he shut himself away in his upper rooms.

When the news of the washed-up bodies came, Hunt, Byron, and Trelawney set out for Viareggio, where temporary burial on the shore had satisfied quarantine rules. With permission to exhume them, Trelawney, with a fine regard for pagan ritual, built a funeral pyre; Hunt stayed in the carriage, grief overwhelming him; Byron swam far out to sea in the searing midday heat. The smoke rose above the glittering sea and the desolate mountains embraced the flames, flaring bright orange with the wine and oil poured over the body.

On the way back to Pisa, Hunt and Byron drowned their sorrows, alcohol obliterating grief and the horror of holding Shelley's blackened heart. Hunt's hopes were wrecked; his reason to be in Italy was gone, his heart broken. Byron soon lost interest in the *Liberal* and took up the cause of Greek independence. Mary, devastated at losing her soulmate, and vulnerable in the early days of widowhood, flirted with Byron, to Hunt's impotent rage. She returned to London where a stage version of *Frankenstein* was planned. Hunt's financial problems earned him a lifetime reputation for debt and borrowing. But his children thrived in the Italian sun, offending their various hosts but deeply

loved by their parents. On the advice of a doctor
Marianne gave birth to Vincent, Leigh's prop in his
old age, until finally penury drove them back to
England, overland, back to London, and their friends.

CHAPTER 17

Virginity Regretted

As the door to the Hunts' house was shut behind them, Charlotte braced herself against the railings of the neighbouring cottage. She faced Will in the darkness.

'I couldn't do it,' she said, letting out a deep breath.

'Neither could I,' replied Will. 'Neither could Hunt. His children thrived because he more or less obeyed the rules—'

'More or less?' said Charlotte sharply.

'Yes, more or less. There was some gossip about his sister-in-law, but I think it was just gossip. You can see what he's like—'

'And you,' she said sternly, ignoring this, 'did you more or less obey the rules?'

He laughed and drew her closer to him. Was she jealous? He hoped so. 'Sadly, more,' he said. 'If you really want to know, in the interests of literature I once ended up in a house of ill repute after discussing a novelist's work and drinking too much. That is all.'

She turned her face away. She hated that whorehouse with all her being.

'Now, Miss Brontë,' he said, mock seriously, 'I think we may have missed the last omnibus. We must get a cab before the night air wreaks havoc with your notorious chest.'

'Those poor children,' she said gruffly. 'Not the Hunts, the others, Shelley's and Byron's – does genius make people so unfeeling?'

'They don't intend it,' said Will. 'They get carried along by the power of their talent, their emotions, their need for love and attention. And the Shelleys were so young, almost children themselves. Byron was different. Incredible ego, complete genius.'

'I loved him when I was young,' said Charlotte quietly. 'Papa let us read him and he became part of our writing. But I didn't realise he had caused such havoc.'

'Are you sure you didn't? Mr Rochester knew about havoc. And Heathcliff was not a saint. Look, we must get a cab or you'll catch cold.'

Suddenly she was decisive. 'No. Let's walk. Do you think you can make it?' She smiled teasingly at him. 'My father walks miles still.'

'Your father my foot,' replied Williams crossly. He hoped she was only trying to prolong their time together. He deliberately quickened his pace as they reached the end of the Cornwall Road and she had to skip a bit to keep up with him. The night was clear, stars sharp as bright pins. The moon, brilliant in the cloudless sky, was nearly full and covered them with a silvery glow, and their breath rose in white streaks as they walked faster.

Julia had unsettled Charlotte: it was not just that she liked her robust attitudes, her brief articulate comments, even her beauty; it was the prospect she presented of things Charlotte had barely dared to think about. 'Still burdened with your virginity, Miss Brontë!' she had laughed. It had seemed so funny in the delivery; but the question, easily answered, made her feel hot, embarrassed. She turned to Will, retrieving her arm, her hands folding into their muff.

'I...' she began.

'Yes?' he countered, in the pause.

'I – oh, no matter,' she said, taking his arm again. 'I was thinking of the Hunts' long marriage and all the children. I think,' she paused, 'I think I would like to have children.'

'Well,' said Will, 'it's certainly a way of passing on your gifts. The writing gift is fairly strong in your family.' He chuckled, taking her arm back, close to him and his warmth. 'Three writing, published daughters! Your parents certainly had the knack!' She glanced at him with slight disapproval. 'Sorry,' he said, 'but you know what I mean. If you want to preserve that gift you'd better get on with it.'

They seemed to have reached a new level of intimacy as well as the environs of Kensington, and cabs were plying for hire. Williams, feeling he may have overstepped the mark, caused a distraction by hailing one. But far from being offended, she was exploring the idea.

'Do you mean Mr Nicholls?'

'Possibly,' he replied. 'You didn't mention children when we started on this project. It was marriage and then love. Now you've seen the Hunts' faithful marriage, with lots of children and,' he smiled disarmingly, 'mine,' she nodded, 'the unorthodox marriages of Thornton Hunt and George Lewes, the passion of Keats, the agony and ecstasy of the poets and their children. Indeed, think about children; they enhance your life like nothing else. And I think you ought to think about marriage without children, what that means; it could happen to you.'

'Because I'm thirty-eight?'

'It could happen, possibly. I'd like you to see a marriage with genius but without children, before you make any decisions about Mr Nicholls.'

The cabdriver was calling to his horse to stop. They were at the boarding house. Williams paid the man and the skinny tired horse moved off, clip-clopping sadly into the darkness. He put his arms around her and hugged her to him. 'No,' he breathed softly, 'don't make any decisions about Mr Nicholls yet.' She lay still against him, then turned up her face to be kissed.

'No, no decisions,' she murmured. 'What next?'

He knocked on the door for the maid to open it, and drew away from her to hand her up the steps respectably.

'The Carlyles. Thomas and Jane. Married more

than twenty years and not a bairn in sight.'

He let go of her hand reluctantly.

***

Letting herself into her peaceful room, she put the candle on the dressing table and pulled off her cloak, unhooked the front of her dress, stepped out of it and removed her stays. The heavy curtains had been drawn by the maid and there was a fire laid in the grate. Feeling cold in just her shift, she picked a spill from the mantelpiece and lit it from the candle, bent down and watched the sticks kindle slowly, then lick the coal. Suddenly she felt exhausted and unpinned her hair to relieve the tightness in her brow. It fell loose on her shoulders and she leaned forward to catch the warmth of the fire, instinctively holding her hair back with one hand from the flames. Papa. He'd always feared fire and taught them to lean away from the flames even if they were cold. Suddenly she had an image of the old man, alone in his study at the Parsonage, noble head thrown back in sleep as he dozed alone through yet another long evening. 'Burdened with your virginity and still living with your father?' Julia's words returned to her urgently.

And why was she? Had she not just heard of poets and writers who had thrown it gladly away? Mary Godwin at sixteen, eloped with her poet, Claire Claremont not much older, seducing Byron and pregnant by him; that woman who Will said could write so well having a tumultuous, loving affair with George Lewes while she, Charlotte Brontë, author of best-selling novels and every bit as good a writer as any of them, still burdened with virginity and living at home. She snatched up her hairbrush and began furiously to beat her hair. And Julia Hunt had spotted it! What on earth was she doing? Here she was in London to ask timorously of Mr Williams how to make up her mind to marry her father's curate? At thirty-eight? And *Mr Nicholls?* Had she wasted her romantic life to end up having only the curate to marry? 'Oh God,' she suddenly exclaimed out loud, hand suspended with the hairbrush in mid-air. 'What have I done?'

What indeed. Rising from the floor, she loosened her shift where it clung to her small, shapely body and climbed into the welcoming feathers of her mattress; she had ended up with no man, no baby, not even allowing herself the comfort of lovers in her fiction. Marian Evans had simply departed from Coventry, gone to London, and life and love had started for her. Mary Godwin had run away with Shelley at sixteen, Claire Claremont had seduced Lord Byron at eighteen; these girls seized life and lovers while she had stayed at home and dropped a little bitterness and disappointment into her novels. And now – she rolled hotly and luxuriously into the feathers – was it too late now that she had found a man she could love and give herself to?

Suddenly she lay still. He was married.

But so was Shelley when Mary met him; so was Byron for Claire; so was George Lewes for Marian Evans, and so was M Heger when Charlotte met him in Brussels. Why had she not seduced him? Byron had let it happen, had said no man could resist the offer. But no, she thought fiercely, burning with the thought of her virginal failure, no, she had gone home and written a book about him! *Can there be a more ridiculous gifted writer than I?*

Sleep came fitfully, and she witnessed the slow growth of light as the dawn came. Standing at the window she raised the sash and leaned out into the cold air. Was it too late? Could she make something of her emotionally chilly life? She thought of Will with longing and love, apprehension and not a little dread.

CHAPTER 18

Mr and Mrs Carlyle

Mrs Smith had gathered from her son George that Charlotte Brontë was in town; their meeting at the Opera and Charlotte's introduction to Miss Blakeway had pleased her, for it was she who had told Charlotte in a letter that her son was engaged to be married. She had not seen Charlotte's rebarbative reply, but had suspected something of the sort. Now that things were so happily settled, she desired to renew acquaintance with the woman who she liked and respected, as long as she didn't marry her son; therefore an invitation was sent with Will for the soirée planned for the next evening. The Smiths had moved into a new, impressive house in Gloucester Terrace, and the purpose of the evening was gently to expose their friends and business contacts to their new, stable prosperity.

When Charlotte heard about the invitation she grimaced, rolling her handkerchief into a ball in her tiny hand.

'Do I have to?'

'I rather think you do.' They were in the sitting room of the boarding house and outside there was one of the worst fogs of the winter. It seeped into the house through doors opened and swiftly closed, windows which didn't fit, and even entered on clothes. When Will had arrived and she had embraced him, she felt the cold on his clothes and smelt the smoky, sooty fog on his coat. 'It would seem rude not to, and I have to go; at least we would be together, I have to take four of my "children". Margaret is still unwell so will not be coming.' There was unspoken relief in the room.

'Will it be full of the great and the good?' she asked, sighing. 'You know how I hate these gatherings. I have offended people before by not being the sparkling wit they all expected me to be, or having beauty and grace.'

'I'll look after you this time,' he said gently. 'I promise to stay close by you and rescue you if I see you're getting desperate. My children will look after themselves so I'll be free to watch over you.' She gave a weak smile and a nod of agreement.

'Just see you do. Or from my last performance I shall go down in history as disagreeable, ugly, and shy.'

She spent a long time making the olive silk worthy of another night out. She ordered the hot water, jugs and bowls necessary for washing her hair and eventually had it dry and glossy. Dividing it carefully from a neat centre parting, she pinned the shining mass at the nape of her neck. She sat before the looking glass and pinched her cheeks until she glowed slightly, then bit her lips; there was little else she could do, she had no cosmetics and knew they would have made her look unnatural. After the debacle with her hairpiece, when the portrait painter had looked at it and asked her to remove her hat, she vowed she would never use anything artificial again. Sprinkling a little lavender water round her neck and ears, she took a last look and pulled a face, just preventing herself from putting out her tongue at her reflection. *Stop it,* she thought. *Emily and Anne are not here now, to laugh with you.* Her eyes filled with tears: how hard it was to be an only child after their long apprenticeship together. She went down the stairs and found Will waiting in the hall. He smiled up at her.

'You look beautiful,' he said, with total sincerity. That was just what she needed, true or not. He was just what she needed, married or not. They went out into the raw, foggy air; there were two carriages waiting, the horses' breath whitening the brown murky air, their harness jingling as they fidgeted and pawed to keep warm. In the second carriage were three of Will's daughters and his eldest son; they leaned out and waved cheerily to Charlotte as their father opened the door of the front carriage, handed her in, then joined her. He knocked on the roof and they were away. It was a slow journey, lamps looming out of the fog, voices shouting to enquire whereabouts.

'This is a great night for George,' said Will, pulling up the window on its worn leather strap to exclude the dirty moisture. 'This new house is much grander than the one you knew in Westbourne Park. It's a measure of his success, and he wants everyone to see the fruits of his work and business. His mother is thrilled.'

'I'm sure she is,' said Charlotte dryly. 'Do all publishers develop souls of brass as they get more successful?'

'Now, now,' said Will, squeezing her hand, 'you have no need of that. You write the books, not him, and everyone here tonight knows that. Publishers make money out of writers, but they can't write the books. And I thought you had put Miss Blakeway behind you.'

'I have indeed,' she replied. She looked longingly at him and her large grey eyes glistened in the darkness. The carriage jolted to a halt. They had arrived at the house in Gloucester Terrace, along with many other carriages. There was a cacophony of horse greetings as their drivers jostled for space. Eventually Williams and Charlotte and his four children were all disgorged onto the pavement, the girls laughing and smoothing their dresses; they had a simple elegance which suited their good looks and disguised their restricted means. Will and his son wore tails and white ties beneath their cloaks, looking handsome and resembling each other markedly. *How good to have children,* she thought. Robert arranged the female company so that he and his father had a woman on each arm.

It was certainly grand, there was no doubt about that; the fine mahogany staircase, adorned with branched candelabra shedding flattering light on all the women, starkly contrasted to Charlotte the modesty of her home and Will's; if she had married George Smith she would have had to put up with his burgeoning wealth and his not entirely tasteful expression of it. At the doors of the spacious drawing room they were greeted by George, his mother, and

Miss Blakeway, who was just as enthusiastic about Charlotte as she had been at the Opera. Mrs Smith was eagerly greeting the Williams children, who had easy, charming manners, complementing their good looks; Charlotte envied them their composure, unintimidated by their surroundings, and greeting with open friendliness the people around them. George bent low to kiss her hand and murmured how glad he was to see her; she was able to look straight at him and be bold in her thanks.

The panels on the walls were papered in a green floral design and framed in gold; the long windows were hung with a fine satin damask, and all the furniture seemed new. On a little dais at the far end musicians perched on fragile gilt chairs played softly. Charlotte wondered if anyone was listening to them. Had George dictated their repertoire? It had a feel of popular ballroom about it, so probably George's choice. This was clearly an evening of the statement of status. She clung harder to Will's arm.

'Now, who are you going to talk to?' he whispered, gesturing towards the room full of people, feathers and silk, fans fluttering, the rising boom and twitter of voices.

'Just don't leave me,' she hissed back. 'I'll put up with whoever you choose!'

Like a homing pigeon he steered her towards a very new velvet upholstered chair on which sat a small, neatly groomed woman with the largest and most startling eyes Charlotte had ever seen. She was by no means young; her raven hair was drawn back and streaked with grey, and her face showed sharp lines with sadness dragging them down further. But she had an air of expectancy, of acerbity, a bird-like vibrancy.

'Och, Mr Williams,' she said, offering a small, well-scrubbed hand. She didn't smile, but her eyes bored into Charlotte mercilessly. 'This is Miss Brontë, is it not? I saw you at Thackeray's some time ago, my dear. Not a happy evening for you, I think. You seem happier now.' The Scottish voice, rolling its Rs and meticulously separating syllables, was instantly attractive. Williams turned to Charlotte.

'May I present Mrs Carlyle?'

Charlotte took a deep breath. 'I am happier,' she said. 'I find large social gatherings complete torture. Mr Williams has kindly undertaken to protect me tonight.' Jane Carlyle suddenly smiled.

'I cannot bear them either!' Her eyes shone. 'Mr Carlyle,' she waved a small imperious hand in the direction of a tall, thin man smoking a long pipe despite the widely accepted custom of not smoking in drawing rooms, and holding forth to a keen circle. 'Mr Carlyle, for a man of *very* (the Rs rolled) democratic views, loves nothing better than to mix with the aristocracy at balls and such like. Last week I had to go practically *nude* to Lady Ashburton's ball. My arms and neck have been securely muffled for years and all of sudden they have to be revealed.' She leant towards Charlotte and touched her with her fan. 'I have to say that by candlelight I did not shame him! But what a trouble to dress; I keep only one servant, and they are constantly leaving.'

'Really?' Will observed a slight smugness cross Charlotte's features. 'We too keep only one, but she has been with us for thirty years.' Jane looked at her keenly.

'D'ye have to do some of the work yourself, then, as I do?' She stretched out her own very clean, short-nailed hand, scrutinised it, then glanced at Charlotte's. 'Over the years I've learned to cook, and clean the grate, take the curtains down, be rid of the bed bugs,' Charlotte gulped, 'do you do all that, Miss Brontë? I was not born to it,' she finished competitively.

'Mostly,' replied Charlotte. 'Our mother died early and we were brought up to help in the house. We lit fires dusted, washed, anything really. We've,' a shadow crossed her face, 'I've learned a few tricks. If visitors arrive early for dinner, I tell them I have a chapter to finish and would they mind talking to my father while I do it? Then I go into the kitchen and finish off the dinner with Tabby.' Jane Carlyle screeched with mirth, then apologised.

'Mr Carlyle calls me his *screamikin*. I try to be quieter but it's not natural to me. Have you any more tricks to teach me, then? Will, bring Miss Brontë to tea with me tomorrow. I only do tea these days.' She turned back to Charlotte. 'I hope you'll come. I had no idea you'd be such good company. You seemed a wee bit gloomy before.' Will agreed to the invitation on Charlotte's nod; he was quite glad to move on as he had not anticipated discussing the servant problem this evening. He moved towards Thackeray's group where the great man stood immensely tall above the acolytes.

Charlotte swerved.

'No!' He looked surprised, but then remembered the unhappy dinner where she appeared to have disappointed the guests. But it wasn't just that.

'You let me do it!' she almost spat at him. 'You let me dedicate the second edition of *Jane Eyre* to him—'

'But only because he's your hero—'

'But *you* knew and *I* didn't that he had a mad wife, and all London thought that because I had been a governess, he was Mr Rochester! You should never have let me do it! Papa was mortified! I can't possibly speak to him.'

Williams held on to her and muttered, 'I know – we were so busy at the time we didn't realise the possibilities.' Privately he thought, *If she still minds that she's never going to weather any scandal about her and me...*

Charlotte surveyed the room; food was now being served and the musicians manfully did their best as the noise rose. The Williams children were seamlessly absorbed by their good manners and cheerful conversation. Charlotte observed them with a mixture of admiration and envy. How wonderful to have grown up children, to be almost like friends with you; such reward for years of care. She knew her father felt like that. He loved their – her – company. Suddenly she was standing with Dickens. Always the centre of attention. He turned round, his black curly hair over his collar, his taut little frame encased in a costly new suit.

'Not come to terms with the serial novel yet, Miss Brontë? Perhaps you don't have the stamina?' Despite Will's presence, she bridled.

'It's not stamina I lack,' she replied coldly, 'it's the idea of my art responding to a weekly deadline, whether I'm able to write my best or not. I might end up sending off second rate copy.'

'We all do it, my dear,' he said cheerfully, 'we all do

it. How else does one make a crust?' Charlotte shoved Will quite hard, and, as the great man was already distracted by the keen looks of various nondescript literary ladies, they were able to escape.

'Insufferable man,' she whispered. 'Where is Mrs Dickens?'

'Pregnant, I expect,' muttered Will. 'Or annoyed at Nellie Ternan.'

'Nellie Ternan?'

'His mistress. He thinks no one knows about her, but we all do.'

Charlotte chuckled. 'That makes me feel better.' She glanced around the splendid room. 'And Mr Lewes away in Weimar, Thackeray's wife incarcerated, and you with me. Is anyone with whom they ought to be?' Will looked across the room.

'Mr and Mrs Carlyle,' he said with a smile.

***

The Thames swirled dark and glittering under the late afternoon sky, catching lamplight here and there, trickling and sucking as boats cleaved the thick water, mud mingling with sewage and debris. There was no embankment near where the Carlyles lived; the work had already started up at Westminster, and would eventually reach Chelsea, bringing with it not only the embankment but untold wonders of sanitation. But for now, the Carlyles were safe in their Queen Anne stronghold, unregenerate and dependent on buckets, mops, coal, and elbow grease. The house was terraced, brick built, imposing, found for them at a reasonable rent in 1834 by Leigh Hunt who had lived round the corner. And here they had stayed for twenty years, becoming Londonised, dyspeptic and famous. Before he knocked on the door, Charlotte steered Will past it and round a corner, wishing to do her homework.

'You said they came from Scotland?'

'Yes, his cleverness attracted him to her as a suitor, although socially she was way above him. She wanted to nurture his genius and then share in his fame, and he was quite happy to be nurtured. It was her idea to come to London, after a few chilly years in the Scottish countryside. Soon after they arrived here he published his *French Revolution* – there's a story there but—'

'Tell me!'

'I warn you, it'll make you cry. He gave the manuscript to his friend John Stuart Mill to read, who left it in a heap on a chair, whereupon his maid lit the fire with it!'

'I'm not crying, my heart's stopped.'

'When he told Carlyle he said he would just start again. What he said to Jane was probably different.' He stopped and twirled his stick to point at a house on the other side of the road. 'That was where the Hunts lived; do you know that poem of Leigh's:

"Jenny kiss'd me when we met,

Jumping from the chair she sat in;

Time, you thief, who love to get

Sweets into your lists, put that in!

Say I'm weary, say I'm sad,

Say that health and wealth have missed me,
Say I'm growing old, but add,
Jenny kiss'd me!'"

He looked at her hard. 'Never realised the truth of that before. I'm growing old, kiss me!' Afterwards, as they walked on, he said, 'Jenny was Jane Carlyle. Men adored her; young, pretty, witty, articulate. The chair she sat in is still there, you'll see it. Like us, they don't change their furniture, even if they go up in the world.'

'You wouldn't be referring to...?'

'Dear old George? Of course not! That's his business. But although Jane loved Leigh, she has had a pretty volatile relationship with Marianne. The words "drunkish" and "devilish" come to mind. By then they had ten children and Marianne was not that well.' They had reached a corner so Will steered them back towards Cheyne Row, pausing under the puttering gaslight. 'She borrowed things and didn't return them, Jane is pretty fastidious and objected to bits of food on the floor and the general disorder. But Marianne gave them the bust of Shelley she sculpted, which is gift enough to make up for everything, in my view. You'll see it in the parlour.'

'Did Mr Carlyle like the Hunts?'

'Yes, he loved Leigh despite the borrowing and he tolerated the children whom he saw as nomadic gipsies. But I think their number rather emphasised the Carlyle's lack, as mine did.'

'Did they want children?'

'Can't say for sure; when the Ruskins' annulment

was in the news there were those who said the reason for that – non-consummation – would apply to the Carlyles, but who can ever know if the parties keep silent? However, in twenty years Jane has changed from a happy, witty woman to a witty but misanthropic hypochondriac. Something has eaten at her. She's always striving to please Mr C. but it's hard. He enjoys being lionised and the company of clever women with big houses, despite his pride in his humble origins. One particularly.' They had arrived back at the tall house. Standing on the steps under the gaslight above the door, Will lifted the lion head door knocker and let it fall twice; their conversation ceased.

The door was answered by a flustered but willing maid, who took their cloaks and hats and disappeared to the nether regions. Jane Carlyle, neat as a flower, her little dog jumping around the visitors, came out of the parlour. 'Hello, lovely dog,' Charlotte murmured as she bent down and scratched him behind the ears; how she loved a dog smell, particularly wet, clean or dirty, although Nero appeared very clean. At home in Haworth there had been a long line of dogs ever since she was a child, varying from Emily's fierce Keeper to Anne's docile Flossie; her father would never be without a dog. She felt at home, unusually relaxed. Mrs Carlyle led them into the parlour.

It was a room hovering between pretty and handsome; the fine windows, high ceilings and panelled folding doors were softened by the delicate floral wallpaper, patterned carpet and a cheerful well heaped fire, in an iron basket, which crackled and spat. Charlotte was guided to a low chair (was this the chair Jenny jumped from?) by a circular table. Will took his seat on the couch where Nero jumped up and nestled by him, encouraged to sit close by his caressing hand. Charlotte longed to join them. Candles lit the room and light flickered in the looking glass above the fire. A room she felt very comfortable in; a room created with love and art.

'What a lovely room,' she said softly, settling her wide skirt around her. Jane smiled her long-lipped smile, not showing her teeth, but the expression in her large black eyes signalled approval. Charlotte felt there was a dangerous light in those eyes, and determined to go carefully.

Taking the tea from the maid Mrs Carlyle settled herself opposite Charlotte, handing her a fine cup and sugared biscuits. Rising from her chair she took his tea over to Will and said in her clear Scottish tones, 'Welcome to our tea partykin. Will you not take your tea up to the new study, Will, to Mr C? He'll be pleased to see you. Just keep climbing the stairs, you'll arrive in the roof if not in heaven.' Will took the hint and deciding that Charlotte could handle one small woman in a pleasant house, disappeared. She could hear his footsteps echoing away up the stairs but did not panic. The room, the fire, the comfortable order and modest comeliness of everything was familiar to her from her own home, and she felt empathetic to Jane Carlyle for a reason not plain to her yet. Despite her reputation for acerbity, for tedious involved stories often featuring the life, times, and catastrophes of her servants, her damning criticism of other people's work while doing nothing herself, she seemed at this time to radiate kindness and sympathy. The pretty voice broke in on her thoughts. 'A great pleasure to have you here, Miss Brontë—'

'Charlotte—'

'Thank you!' She had come back to sit by the fire. 'Charlotte – this is an unexpected visit, is it not? We generally know who is coming and going in London, Mr C. always has an ear to the ground and I don't like to miss a thing! Are you here about your writing? Is it the next book after *Villette*?'

'No. I came to see Will, Mr Williams,' she corrected herself hastily, knowing well that this astute and experienced woman would pick up any intimacy. 'I needed to—' And suddenly, alarmingly, against her lifetime's practice, it all came tumbling out, her need to understand marriage and make a decision about Mr Nicholls, her isolation after the deaths of Branwell, Emily, and Anne, her fear of loneliness after her father's inevitable death. She looked at Jane Carlyle with glistening eyes and found reciprocal tears there.

'My dear,' she whispered, leaning across to take Charlotte's hand, 'my dear, you are suffering. That I know about, and I know about marriage!' She withdrew her hand and gazed into the fire, her sad face shadowed in its flickering light. She paused a moment as the coals shifted and fell into ash. 'Let me tell you about marriage, but first tell me about Mr Nicholls.' They faced each other, eye to eye, trust deepening into intimacy.

'He's my father's curate, you know I've made jokes at the expense of curates in *Shirley*. But we did rather suffer from curates during our childhoods, three daughters in the house meant there was always one of them taking a romantic interest in us, and the possibility that it might help Papa as he grew old if one of them married one of us and helped to keep on the perpetual curacy Papa holds. That would have kept the Parsonage safe for all of us. But now there's just me and him, and the Reverend Arthur Nicholls wants to marry me. He's kind, and thoughtful; pleasant looking; quite intelligent; but Papa thinks he is beneath me—'

'Aha!' cried Jane, delightedly. 'That was exactly how it was with me and Mr Carlyle! I was the doctor's daughter, "the flower of Haddington" they called me, and he was of peasant stock. His dear old mother still can't read and write! But he was clever beyond imagination and was at university with my old tutor. Now there's a story.' Charlotte had heard that Mrs Carlyle could talk uninterrupted, and well, for minutes on end, making a comic anecdote out of a scrubbing brush, although Mr Carlyle had rivalled her by managing three hours without stopping. She wondered how long this diversion would be, but decided to see what happened. She felt comfortable, and content in the knowledge that Will was upstairs with The Sage; as long as he was close she was happy.

'The story being that I was deeply in love with Mr Irvine, my tutor, but he was promised to another and of such honour that he would not consider breaking it off.' She looked stricken for a moment as she contemplated her loss. 'And so I married Mr C.' Abruptly she rose and went to the couch where Nero lay, belly up, paws aloft; gathering the four paws together in one hand she bent and kissed his neck. 'Perhaps I wouldn't be so fond of the dog had I married Mr Irvine, Charlotte. It's been a lonely old road. Have you had other lovers?'

'Yes,' she replied, quite forcefully, 'three proposals besides Mr Nicholls.'

"Four! And they all proposed marriage?' Charlotte nodded. 'You're a braw wee girl! I had no idea!' She regarded Charlotte with increased interest, thinking of the unflattering things that had been said about her and her appearance on previous visits. Clearly there were hidden depths. 'But don't think that marrying your curate will stop you being lonely. I've been married to Mr C. for over thirty years and been alone and lonely for much of it. If he's not writing his books, preoccupied and unattainable, needing his illnesses monitored and his special food cooked, then he's travelling to his relatives, and if she's in town he's every night at Bath House, he must have walked thousands of miles to it over the years, or down in her country house.'

'Her?"

'Lady Ashburton!' Jane fairly hissed the name and returned to the fire. Gathering her skirts near to her she sat on her hands, as if she didn't trust them not to commit some barbarism on Lady Ashburton. 'He's been fairly mesmerised by the woman for years and years. She's as rich as Croesus, and gathers writers, artists, politicians, bankers around here in her great houses. She tries to be nice to me so that he keeps going to her, but she needn't bother because he'd go anyway.'

'Is she married?' asked Charlotte, anticipating another revelation from the London literary scene, perhaps one she could surprise Will with.

'Yes, yes, she's married, but it's not *like that*.' She stopped, drew breath and started again. *'He's* not like that. He never has been.' She glanced at the closed door and lowered her voice. 'I'll tell you this because I don't want you making wrong decisions, my dear, and you're discreet, and I can trust you.' She cocked her head to one side and raised her eyebrows. Charlotte nodded vigorously. She needed this conversation to go seamlessly on. Jane looked at her fondly. 'I'd have loved a daughter like you, and her bairns too to care for. With Mr C. and me for parents she might well have been a writer. But—' She shifted uneasily in her seat, as if unsure whether to continue. Charlotte held her breath and willed her on. 'But he's not like – that – and never has been. When we were young I felt I could do anything, I learned Latin and mathematics and languages, that's why he loved me, and then when I had to I learned to cook and bake bread and manage the money and clean the house and light the fires. But I could not, *could not*,' she repeated, bringing her fist down on her knee, 'I could not get him to give me a bairn.'

Audaciously Charlotte murmured, 'Not ever?'

'No, not ever. Hardly a kiss, hardly a hug. I have wept nights and nights away while he paced the house complaining about sleeplessness. Perhaps if he – had – had – he would have slept better!'

Silence reigned in the room. The candles puttered and Charlotte stole a look at Jane; tears were sliding down her cheeks. She took her hand between both of hers.

'I'm sorry.'

'Don't be. It's over, the longing and the hoping. Now I have the dog. I need someone, something to look after.' She called the dog to her, and Nero leapt across the room and landed in her lap. 'There's Nero, and I think I smother the servants, that's why they leave, or drink, and Mr C. is never without biliousness, or headache or constipation, and the noise! My dear, he cannot stand cockerels, or wind, or the piano next door, or the organ grinder in the street, or chickens, or the parrot in the garden, or the street sellers.' Charlotte burst out laughing.

'So what do you do?'

'Well, I've spent most of this year having a soundproof room for his study,' she whispered melodramatically, 'constructed in the roof. *Anything* to stop the complaints. He has been away, in Scotland or with Lady A.,' she grimaced, 'so he has had no disruption, no noise, but to complete this project I have had to sleep on the sofa, in his bed, in my bed and eaten nothing because we couldn't cook, and when he came home all he could say was that the workmanship was shoddy and he could still hear the hooters on the river and the birds! While he's away he writes to me and tells me how he loves me and how happy I make him, but when he's here he never says any such thing. Recently he wrote of "the misery that we are in." But I love him. I want him to love me, not the ladies who lionise him. I never thought he would be vain enough to fall for all this spurious attention. It's not what we were brought up to.' She stopped and Charlotte could hear the tears again in her voice. She imagined the young Carlyles, all dutiful thrift and lack of vanity, changed over the years into adored lion and seething slave. 'We lived for six years in a Scottish desert called Craigenputtock, where he worked on his *Sartor Resartus*, sixteen miles in either direction to the nearest habitation, so quiet you could hear the sheep nibbling the grass when the wind didn't drown them. And him locked away writing or walking for his health, and he did not, most definitely did not, want company on his walks. He was thinking.' She sighed exasperatedly, the memory so fresh and vivid. 'Each book takes *years* – when we came to London we had to live on very little as he had no income, and then he started the lectures to which practically the whole of London came, and suddenly we had money. I thought things might change then; they did, we had more money and more society, but no bairns or the making of them.' She blushed. 'I should not have said that. It's indelicate. You'll think I'm like the women here who run off with men like Mr Lewes.' Charlotte took another risk.

'Did you never have any special friends?'

'If you mean men, certainly not. That's not how I was brought up. Leigh Hunt loved me in the early days, wrote me poems, flirted and ate an enormous amount of porridge at my fireside—'

Charlotte interrupted: 'He still eats porridge!'

Jane laughed, cheered. 'But all this does not solve your problem. You don't need a man to keep you, you're a woman of means, Charlotte, you don't need a man for money, and your reputation will mean people will come flocking to your door so I doubt you'll be lonely, despite your fears. You could move to London and have a salon! But children, what wouldn't I have given for children, and there's only one way to achieve them. They might have softened the edges of Mr C., it would have done him good not to have me dancing attendance on him – if you think he'll give you children, and that's what you want, then marry him. But be sure he will!'

'How can I possibly be sure?' She echoed Jane. 'That's not how I've been brought up!'

'Well, when I had Mr Irvine interested in me I could tell when he was close to me, just standing by me, there was warmth in him and I knew that if I had touched his hand he would have responded, and I had a response to him, an electricity which sort of – thrilled me. With Mr C. I was too busy prattling on, mistaking our conversations for love and revelling in how clever he was that I forgot to check the essential. He was – is still, cold, unresponsive. I fell in love with the song, not the singer. We women know so little. I had no idea what to expect and was always thinking something would happen, expecting it would come from somewhere as time went on. How was I to know what was normal, what usually happened? Just check Mr Nicholls' electricity with your own, Charlotte, however modestly.'

Night had fallen and Jane went to the windows to draw the curtains. Footsteps echoed on the stairs and there was a discreet tap on the closed door. Will came in, alert to any tension in the room. He found the two women in surprising harmony, both with colour in their cheeks. The dog raised an ear at him as if to say, *I could tell you a thing or two but I won't.*

'He's a dry old stick,' he said to Charlotte as they walked back by the river. 'Of course I respect his work, but he does go on. I don't think I said more than three words while I was up there. First we had the history of the soundproof study, and how it isn't, then his delicate health, then the problems of writing Frederick the Great which he reckons will take sixteen years in all. What did you and Mrs Carlyle talk about?'

'Oh, this and that,' said Charlotte vaguely. 'Just this and that.'

CHAPTER 19

Decisions

Charlotte found packing her bag more difficult than it had been when she fled from Haworth; there were three books which Will had given her from Smith Elder's generous stocks, and the violets he had bought her from a tattered old woman in the street which she had pressed between the pages of her novel. She had bought some of the best steel pens made, wrapped and tied carefully in brown paper, some for herself, some to give to her father, although his failing sight restricted his writing these days to parish records, and he was still wedded to the quill which he could sharpen skilfully, gently feeling the developing point when his eyes failed him in the dim light of winter. She had indulged herself with a fine woollen shawl, rich with autumn colours swirled into a circular design, and big enough to envelope most of her small body when she needed an extra layer to escape the piercing draughts which whistled through the Parsonage despite the best efforts of carpenters and builders to stop their incessant whine. She had bought it in an emporium in Oxford Street, fascinated by the vast space which sold everything at different counters designed to display and tempt newly prosperous shoppers. She had wanted to buy a present for Will, but she was confused by their new intimacy. It was odd, she thought, how one wants to give presents to those one is in love with – she remembered netting a watch case and decorating it with her finest embroidery for Monsieur Heger. With a little judicious pressing and pulling she at last had stowed it all alongside her own things. She was dressed in her heavy travelling dress and her cloak. She had abandoned the muff for gloves to free her hands for the journey.

She looked around the room with regret; although she had her own room at home, and the dining room to work in, the reminders were all too palpable: the couch where Emily lay daily for three months until she allowed Papa to summon the doctor when all hope was gone; the fireside where they had all gathered as children while he read aloud to them the transactions of Parliament from the newspaper; and, worst of all, the echoing feet of her sisters as they tramped nightly round the table together, beating harder on floor boards, softer on carpet, discussing their work, reading it aloud. Now she walked alone, waiting for her father to open the door and say, 'Don't sit up too late, Charlotte,' at nine o'clock. He used to say 'girls'. She shuddered. In this anonymous London bedroom she could forget all that and remember only the awakening she had felt since coming to London, surprised by love which she had not sought but could not relinquish. If she was confused on arrival, she was overwhelmed on departure.

They had decided to eat together before she caught her train back to the north. Will was concerned that she had to face the long journey alone, through the night. His heart was too full to tell her how and why he yearned to protect and love her, knowing as he did that there was little he could do but revert to the correspondent she had relied on for so many years. They took a cab to Verrey's in Regent Street, recommended to Charlotte by Jane Carlyle as a restaurant even a single woman could eat in. She had been there herself, when her house was in disorder to create the soundproof study, Mr C. was absent living in luxury at Lady Ashburton's, and they were between maids. She had, she said, consumed a very good chop and a glass of ale for a very reasonable price.

Will, with the ease of a Londoner, had arranged a discreet table away from the door and the noise of customers entering and departing. It was indeed a respectable establishment; he could imagine Mrs Carlyle, dour and dyspeptic, observing the other diners for material for some anecdote, treating the waiters without familiarity yet compelling their constant attention. The room was redolent of a chop house rather than a superior restaurant, halfway between a men's club and one's own home. The walls were panelled, the table linen sparkling white, the lighting adequate but flattering, and among the diners there were indeed some lone women, treated courteously and unembarrassed. *Governesses*, thought Charlotte, *on their half day off; or women living alone in lodgings where the evening meal was only provided five days a week. Enough to drive me into the arms of Mr Nicholls as I can't have Will.* But no; she had money, she still had Papa, if she married it must be for what *she* wanted. That much she had certainly learned since she arrived in London. She paused in her reverie and casually reached for Will's hand across the table.

'We both know what we can't have,' she started slowly, 'so shall we start from there?'

'And then talk about what we can?' he countered. She sighed deeply, leaving one hand in his and leaning her face on the other, so that it was difficult to read her expression. Her hair shone in the candle light, and he felt she looked better, brighter, even plumper than when she arrived a few days ago. If Lewes and Thackeray, who had been so uncomplimentary about her looks, could see her now, he thought, they would have been surprised at how this glow transformed her. 'We're not adulterers, or elopers,' he continued, 'not even Jane Eyre fleeing from Mr Rochester's proposal that she becomes his mistress—'

'That's a tempting one,' said Charlotte thoughtfully, 'but I don't see it fitting in with either of our families.'

'But we are passionate people who love each other, much more than friends, incipient lovers constrained by circumstances.'

Charlotte nodded, then, looking straight at him, began.

'I have a confession to make. When I came to London this time it wasn't just about Mr Nicholls.' Will raised his shaggy greying eyebrows, revealing more clearly his startling blue eyes.

She was blushing very slightly. 'I came partly because you didn't write to me for the greater part of last year.' Her voice trembled. 'You'd written to me for such a long time, I'd come to rely on your letters, your ideas about my work, about London, other writers; my imagination had started to invest you with more importance than you ever intended. You were mature, clever, understood about this wrestle with words, you were kind to me when Branwell died, and then Emily and Anne. I had never had such a bad time in my life, and you were there, letters arriving regularly. I waited for years for Monsieur Heger to write, when I was in love with him, and he never did. In my mind, you had a kinder character than he, and then it suddenly stopped.'

Will looked devastated. 'But that was because you were in such correspondence with George about *Villette*! I thought you loved him. My feelings for you had grown ever since we first met in London. To me there was always a possibility that you and he might marry. I didn't want to compromise or confuse you with my subjective feelings. I saw myself as an old married man, with exquisite taste in literature my sole virtue; a mere footnote in biography and criticism as the man who discovered *Jane Eyre*.'

'You certainly deserve that,' said Charlotte. 'You changed my life; without your belief in my work I might still be governessing in Yorkshire.' She pulled a gruesome face. 'And now you've changed it again.' The waiter, who had been hovering courteously, caught Will's eye and he ordered soup, fish, small steaks, a light pudding. He'd noticed how much better Charlotte had been eating, compared with her other times in London. 'So I really came about George, and Mr Nicholls, who I could talk about, and you, who I could not.' She shivered slightly. 'I was relieved when I detected your reciprocal feelings.' Will covered her tiny hands in both of his.

'Remember love is an ever fixed mark,' he said quietly. 'Remember that although we cannot be together we can live in each other's hearts.' The soup arrived and she waited spellbound for his next words. 'Whatever happens – who you marry, me living the rest of my life with dear Margaret, nothing will alter what we have now.' Charlotte lifted her spoon and admired the reflections in its upturned bowl, before continuing.

'I don't think I have ever been so happy as I have been these past few days. Oh yes, anxious, regretful, frustrated, all those things, but so happy being with you and talking, talking, talking, feeling you close to me, hearing you laugh. This I can take away with me for the rest of my life.' He smiled and for a moment their attention to the soup, a grey and glutinous concoction, tested their skills against the shining white tablecloth. 'I know now what I want – my ideal, but I know it can't be you.'

'What's the ideal?' he asked with amusement. It had to wait as the fish arrived, plates were exchanged, crumbs brushed away and their intimacy restored.

'I would like to marry someone who loves me with the passion of Keats, the excitement and brilliance of George Lewes, and the fidelity of Leigh Hunt. I think I've got beyond the volatile youth of the Shelleys, and Byron, much as I love the poetry, would lead me a terrible dance and I'd become bitter and tetchy. You know what I'm like.'

'Indeed!'

'And I'd like to have children, like yours, handsome, clever, confident. Do you think I will find all that in Mr Nicholls?'

'You know Mr Nicholls; I don't.'

'He's poor, that's part of the objection; Papa fears poverty from his childhood, but if I never earned a penny more we'd have enough and to spare. He's a good man, but not terribly bright, and has no idea at all about literature. Could I live with that? All my life I've had Papa, who has a brilliant mind, has written and published poetry and gave us unfettered access to literature of all sorts, even Byron!'

'Your father looms large in your life, perhaps he's influencing your choices. Is he impossible to eliminate? You want an older man who loves you unconditionally, with a good mind, fine tastes in literature, and a proven ability to father children?'

'Like you.' A governess rose from her isolated table and was accompanied to the door by a smiling waiter. Charlotte's eyes followed her and then returned to gaze at Will. 'I don't want that woman's life. She's going back to a small bedroom where she guards her few belongings, and to naughty children who she might end up tying to their chairs like my poor sister Anne did. I think I have to marry.' Will sighed like a furnace but nodded in agreement.

'What did Jane Carlyle say to you?' Charlotte laughed as she leaned back to allow the waiter access to their plates. Time was drawing away too quickly; next the meat, soon her departure.

'You were intrigued by our empathy, weren't you?

She warned me about childlessness, its causes and consequences, and coldness. She more or less said that she and Mr C. had never, ever – ever, you know what we will never do.' She sighed, puffing out her lips. 'Why is it that when I find a man I can love that he's married with eight children, and we're both too honourable to do a Lewes? Mrs Carlyle had loved another before Mr C., and regretted losing him for reasons of honour – a bit like us.' She smiled. 'So she married Mr C. without realising she was marrying the idea of genius, and she failed to recognise that he lacked sexual allure, so it seems they are childless because it takes love,' she cleared her throat quietly, 'to make a child.'

'Oh,' said Will, 'so the rumour about the similarity to the Ruskins' annulment is right? What a pity she didn't have a Millais to carry her off.'

'Seems so. She encouraged me to test Mr Nicholls for warmth and...' Her voice trailed away.

'And how do you intend to do that?' Will's question hovered between amusement and jealousy.

'Don't know. And I haven't decided to marry him yet. There's a lot to give up if it doesn't work.'

When the odd-shaped pudding arrived, a sort of milky blob of unknown ingredients, they decided to suspend Mr Nicholls and speak only of literature, love, and the longing they anticipated in the future. Gradually they fell into silence; the restaurant's clients departed singly or in pairs; the waiters spoke softly to each other, and one of them pulled the bolt discreetly on the door so that entrance from the street was not possible. Suddenly they became aware of the empty room, the silence; he raised a hand and the bill arrived and was swiftly despatched. His surtout and her cloak and bag arrived from behind a velvet curtain. Soon they were out in the street, the cold air striking sharply after the warmth within. With her bag in one hand and her on his other arm, he somehow managed to summon a cab.

Leaning back into the fusty leather, she said sadly, 'We're back where we started. Back to the station. Before we had the time all before us, all the possibilities, now it's gone and we'll part forever.' She clung to him and he put his arms round her, hugging her so close she could hardly breathe against him. He kissed her, tasting the salt tears, knowing that he would never do it again in such privacy as the cab afforded. Her response was total, immediate, warm without restraint, realising the finality. Rattled around by the cab on cobbles, they clung together, like young lovers, astonished by the strength of their passion and desolated by the future. At Euston the cab stopped and the burly driver, with downturned mouth and shrugging shoulders, gazed at them, perplexed by their age and the scene he had witnessed in the hidden mirror designed to alert him to crime.

'All right, guv'nor?' he asked, impelled to help with the bag by his curiosity. Will nodded, tipped him well and standing up straight in the cold air, supporting Charlotte and her bag, gazed with tenderness at her tear-streaked face. She turned away, glove becoming handkerchief, then turned back.

'Let's go,' she said. 'Partings are not sweet sorrow. They're absolute hell, they're like death and I've had enough of that.' They were moving rapidly up the platform, pace established by her swift steps, almost dragging Will behind her. How gladly he would have loitered, stretching out these last minutes, just to catch last glimpses of the face he now loved so well. 'Come *on*,' she insisted, and before he knew it they were by the steaming monster of a train, carriage doors opening and shutting, hootings and whistlings, porters' cries and the general cacophony of departure which filled them with an aching sadness. She swung herself up the steps of a carriage which had a well-trimmed oil lamp: ever practical, she knew she would want to read, and slammed the door, creating a barrier between them.

Will, somewhat nonplussed by her haste, stood before her, expectant, then taking gently the hands which were gripping the edge of the lowered window, said, 'Just remember that I love you and will as long as I breathe.' For a moment her sad face relaxed into a half smile.

'That's very literary, Mr Williams. And I will love you, whoever I marry.' The whistle again. Did they blow twice or three times before final departure? 'Don't write anymore. I couldn't bear it. But I'll make sure you know what happens.' Had she then already decided? His thudding heart contracted. Stepping onto the running board, he seized her and kissed her one last time, just as the train moved off. He ran beside, holding one hand, until speed defeated him. He fell back, waving, waving at the tiny figure disappearing, fluttering a handkerchief. Snaking out of the station, the train disappeared in the distance to a pinhead.

***

Six months later, they both received wedding cards.

George, always in early, bristling with energy inside his well-cut suit, had his out already and waved it quizzically at Will as he appeared for the customary morning greeting.

'Miss Brontë's changed her name!' he said. 'It's Nicholls now. Did you know this was afoot, Will?' Will removed his hat and surveyed it minutely with his head down, to hide the shock he felt. They had agreed not to write; he had missed her every day and hoped a manuscript or some attempt at communication would arrive on his desk. And it had. The wedding card, giving the bride's new name, the date of the marriage, and various other appropriate pieces of information about the happy couple, was duplicated to him. He muttered something noncommittal to George about "a possibility" and went to look at his own card. Nothing on it except the printing. No special message in her familiar handwriting. But they had promised, and neither of them would have felt comfortable with deceit. The shortest message between then would have opened the floodgates.

Sitting at his desk he opened yet another brown paper package from a hopeful novelist. Leaning back in his chair he balanced his pencil on his outstretched fingers, then screwed up some waste paper and aimed it at the wicker basket. A shaft of sunlight filtered from the skylight above, shining on the dancing motes of dust that were the inevitable companions of his trade. So she had gone for Mr Nicholls in the end. It was six months since she had been in London with him, so no hasty decision. And Mr Nicholls? Safe, dependable, not clever, without literary tastes, able to father the children she had desired and to help her father. Always her father; perhaps he was her ideal. He hoped fervently that she was happy; suffering at the hands of a demanding, dull, or even selfish man would be more than he could bear to think of.

When his dinner hour came round he had read a few pages of an indifferent novel and written a short contract for a better one. Scraping his chair back, he walked out into the mild June air, wondering how she had looked at her wedding; had she kept the glow that had grown when they were together, or was she again thin, pale, and tense? He had felt proud that she blossomed because they loved each other; now he was in agony that she might blossom for Mr Nicholls. He reached into his pocket and took out a rare cigar for comfort, and, as the smoke curled upwards, walked down to the churning river and stood where they had been together.

***

The months that followed the announcement of the marriage of the Reverend and Mrs Arthur Bell Nicholls passed with little excitement in Smith Elder. George, newly married to Miss Blakeway, was a little less driven and worked slightly shorter hours; Will, unable to resist the lure of discovering new authors, worked hard and tried to dissipate his longing for his twin soul. He attended John Chapman's soirées, missing the convivial company of George Lewes who was still abroad with Miss Evans, watching Dickens with amusement as he presented his respectable domestic facade. The winter came on; London, smothered in the dirtiest fog imaginable, held few other attractions for him, although he still reviewed plays for the extra guineas he gained for his talented children's schooling and music lessons. He walked miles to and from his home, quenching his sorrow by avoiding the omnibus and the memory of Charlotte running up the stairs. He worked hard and late, bearing the concerned enquiries about his health from his wife and daughters with polite dismissal. He wondered, oh how he wondered, how it was all going.

One morning on a cold April day, George came through to his office, ashen and astonished.

'Look at this,' he said. On the desk he put a letter. 'It's from a Yorkshire busy body who used to sell the Brontë sisters paper to write on. He wonders if I have heard of Charlotte's death!'

Words left Will; he could not respond. George paced round the room, passing the letter from hand to hand, rereading, finally putting it in front of Will. Gingerly, he drew it towards him, moving the oil lamp nearer to see more clearly, longing for there to be a mistake, perhaps a hasty misreading by George, missing a vital word which altered the sense. In the pool of light he read quite clearly that Mrs Nicholls had died two days before: that the village thought that she was, as the writer put it, in an interesting condition; that she was very ill during the last weeks, unable to eat or retain food. Her father – *Still there,* thought Will – and her widower were distraught.

He pushed his chair back, ran his hands through his nearly white hair; his face was drained of blood.

'Do you mind,' he said deliberately to George, 'if I just go out for a bit?' George, not surprised at the effect this news had had on Will, waved his arms in a silent gesture of consent.

A chilling wind enveloped him, despite the sun which shone fitfully with all the uncertainty of April. London looked beautiful in the shifting light, grey clouds tipped with sudden light revealing, then hiding, the new buildings, white stone, darker roofs, glittering glass. He left the office and struck out towards the river, following its curve at a swift pace, seeing little for the tears which blurred his vision. So she had gone for children with Mr Nicholls. How high her hopes must have been when she knew she was expecting her baby. Her vision of having grown up children like his had been very real to her, although, and he had to smile at this, wiping a tear away, she had little idea of the gruelling road to get there. They had often talked of the fact that if she died childless there would be no more Brontës, that the unfailing fertility of her father's family would die. Certainly no more Brontës, for Papa had taken the name from Nelson, as he struggled to fit in at Cambridge; all his Irish brothers were called Brunty.

Without realising the distance he had covered, Will found himself on the Chelsea shore, near the Carlyles' house. There was a bench near the river, and despite the sharp wind he sat down, pulling his coat around him. They had paused here before going to the Carlyles', and Charlotte had been fascinated by the setting sun and the skyline, the fast-flowing river and the little boys in the mud, trying to find things to sell. A great ache took hold of him, shuddering through him as his grief spread and emptiness gripped him. This was going to be difficult, covering up his grief, making it modest as an editor should have for a writer. He felt an overpowering need for comfort, to talk about her, the need to talk to someone who had known her, liked her, empathised. Rising to his feet somewhat unsteadily, he walked towards Cheyne Row, and lifted the lion's head knocker. Mrs Carlyle opened the door herself, clad in a tartan shawl. She caught his look of surprise.

'Och, we're between maids again, Will,' she said apologetically, and Mr C. is away.' She beckoned him in, into the parlour. 'It's a good thing I can light a fire myself.' She paused, door handle in hand. 'My dear, whatever is the matter?' She had looked again into Will's face and seen the grief which was now etched by the wind into deep lines. She drew him onto the couch where Nero lay sleeping, taking his hands in hers. 'Tell me.'

And so, sitting in the room where Charlotte had sat, he told her, and his tears shone in the April sunshine which chequered the room through the tall windows; he told her, pouring out his sorrow as Charlotte had poured out her secrets, living through the joy they had had, the mutuality of their souls and their love which would never end.

CHAPTER 20

Loose ends, for those who like to know what happened next

Charlotte Brontë married Mr Nicholls in July 1854. After a honeymoon in Ireland they returned to live with her father in Haworth; he carried out Mr Brontë's parish duties, and she did not write any more. She died after nine months of marriage from excessive pregnancy sickness in March 1855.

Arthur Bell Nicholls stayed with Mr Brontë, doing parish duties until Mr Brontë died in 1861. The parish Trustees then refused to appoint him to Mr Brontë's post. He returned to Ireland, gave up the church and farmed. He died in 1906, when his second wife found in a wardrobe the portrait of the three sisters by Branwell Brontë which now hangs in the National Portrait Gallery, still bearing the creases from its long travel and storage.

William Smith Williams remained at Smith Elder for the rest of his working life, discovering talent and meticulously editing and nurturing it. He retired in 1875 and died six months later. Of his children, Anna is the most famous; she became a professional singer and latterly a Professor at the Royal College of Music. Margaret married the portrait painter Lowes CatoDickinson, and their son Goldsworthy was an advocate in the League of Nations; and to come really up to date, another son Arthur was a senior partner in Price Waterhouse, the London accountants. Williams became related by marriage to the painter Sir Lawrence Alma-Tadema and the writer Edmund Gosse.

George Smith's ambitions were fulfilled at the publishing house of Smith Elder. He gathered writers like George Eliot, Thackeray, Browning, Wilkie Collins, Mrs Gaskell, and Queen Victoria *(Leaves from the Journal of our life in the Highlands)*. He paid most of them far more than he ever paid Charlotte Brontë. He founded the *Cornhill Magazine* and spent lavishly on it, hiring Thackeray as the editor. He was the publisher and main contributor to the *Dictionary of National Biography,* and a tablet in St Paul's Cathedral records that his "warmth of heart endeared him to men of letters". When asked if he had been in love with Charlotte, he said no, he liked her, but better when she was in Yorkshire and he was in London. He died in 1901.

Taylor and Hessey continued to publish poetry and encourage poets. John Clare, a frequent visitor to the Fleet Street premises, was "excellent company while he staid, but a little too much elated with a Glass of Ale if you indulged him with it." After the successes of Keats, Clare, de Quincey, and Thomas Hood, the publishing house failed to thrive and the partnership, but not the friendship, was dissolved, soon after taking on Thomas Carlyle. However, when the new University of London appointed a "Bookseller", that bookseller was John Taylor.

Marian Evans became best-selling novelist George Eliot. She lived with George Henry Lewes for twenty-five years. He encouraged her writing of fiction, acting as her business manager. They seem to have been happy, although after he died her diary records, "Crisis!", sometimes thought to refer to a revelation in his papers. Six months after he died she married John Cross, an accountant twenty years younger than she.

George Henry Lewes was never able marry George Eliot as he could not divorce Agnes having accepted her illegitimate children by Thornton Hunt on their birth certificates, thus condoning the adultery. He published his biography of Goethe in 1855, then began scientific studies which culminated in *The Physiology of Modern Life, Sea Side Studies* and *The Psychology of Mind and Life*. He had papers read at the British Association for the Advancement of Science, and became a fellow of the Zoological Gardens. He wrote extensively in the periodicals of the day, including George Smith's *Cornhill Magazine;* his reputation as a literary critic survives to this day.

Agnes Lewes lived to be eighty years old. Her last child by Thornton Hunt was born in the house where William Smith Williams lived, in Campden Hill Terrace, after the Williamses moved to Canonbury. She was well supported by her husband, and by George Eliot after his death; she died in this house in 1902.

Thornton Hunt was married to Katharine Gliddon and had, counting those with Agnes Lewes, in total fourteen children. During his journalistic career, he co-founded *The Liberal* with Lewes, edited *The Spectator* and was editor of *The Daily Telegraph* from 1855-1873 (his death). He was close to Liberal politicians, particularly Palmerston and Gladstone, and was part of the Association to Repeal a Tax on Knowledge. He is buried next to his father, to whom he remained close, in Kensal Green Cemetery,

Leigh Hunt died in 1859, aged seventy-five. Sadly, he is mainly remembered today for the unkind representation of him as Harold Skimpole in *Bleak House*, and for a few poems, particularly *Jenny kiss'd me* and *Abu Ben Adhem*. Dickens was widely criticised for the Skimpole sketch and eventually apologised. The literary luminaries of the nineteenth century burned so bright that Hunt's literary and humane qualities were cast into shadow, but he did for Keats and Shelley what many others should have done. "Write me as one who loves his fellow men", he wrote.

Marianne Hunt died in January 1857 aged seventy. Hunt was loyal to her to the end, describing her as "generous" and "uncomplaining". After she died it became apparent that she had borrowed money without his knowledge which would have to be repaid from his small income. Despite alcoholism and ill health she retained the affection of her children.

Julia Hunt is not well documented, except for her musical talent and the fact that she never married. She too appears in *Bleak House,* as one of Skimpole's daughters, Comedy.

Lord Byron took up the cause of Greek independence from the Ottoman Empire after he left Italy in 1823, and spent vast sums of money re-fitting the Greek navy. He took part of the rebel army under his own command, despite having no military experience. He became ill, and according to the medical custom of the time, was bled copiously, developing sepsis from which he died in 1824 aged thirty-six. No doubt his difficult early life bred his various failings, but one of our best and wittiest poets.

Mary Shelley returned to England with her son Percy and continued to write, although none of her works had the success of *Frankenstein*. She worked hard to promote Shelley's works and assure his place in literary history. She died aged fifty-one and is buried with the cremated remains of Shelley's heart, and her parents, in Bournemouth.

Claire Clairmont held Byron responsible for the death of their daughter, Allegra, and hated him for the rest of her long life. From Italy she went first to her brother in Vienna, then to Russia as a governess; Russian suitors commented that she treated men with disdain. She worked as a music teacher in England, then lived in Paris, Dresden and finally Florence with her niece. She died in 1879 aged eighty, unmarried.

Jane Carlyle's life continued unhappily until she died in 1866. Carlyle was away in Scotland; she was alone in a carriage with a new little dog for company. She had endured increasingly bad health, but recovered enough from time to time to go to parties.

Thomas Carlyle outlived Jane by twenty years, remaining in the house in Cheyne Row until he died in 1881. He finished Frederick the Great in 1865 the year before Jane died, after sixteen years toil. Its mixed reception did not improve his mental state.

John Ruskin and his wife Effie Gray were granted an annulment of their marriage on the grounds of non-consummation. Effie married the painter John Millais and bore him eight children.

Lady Ashburton pre-deceased Jane Carlyle when she died in Paris in 1857. Thomas Carlyle found her "irreplaceable".

Nero died in 1857. His health declined after he was run over by a butcher's cart, making him look like "a crushed spider" in Jane's words. He died the next year and is buried in Jane's favourite piece of garden at the house in Cheyne Row.

The goat did not return to England from Italy, it seems; warmed by the Italian sun, she may have produced a few kids, like her owners.